Double
Cougar
Trouble

Heart of the Cougar
Book 4

TERRY SPEAR

ISBN-10: 1540612937
ISBN-13: 978-1540612939:

PUBLISHED BY:
Terry Spear

Double Cougar Trouble
Copyright © 2016 by Terry Spear

Discover more about Terry Spear at:
http://www.terryspear.com/

DEDICATION

This book is dedicated to Elizabeth Gaasenbeek. May your dreams come true in everything you do.

ACKNOWLEDGMENTS

Thanks so much to Donna Fournier who helps me so much on brainstorming and keeping me straight on cougar bible matters! And to Dottie Jones and Donna Fournier for making the book even better!

PROLOGUE

Jack Barrington and Dottie Hamilton weren't looking for anything more than a hook-up when he'd met her at an Irish pub off-campus three months ago—a day of carefree fun, sex, and running as cougars through the Ozarks, nothing more. She was a pretty brunette with dark green eyes, a seductive smile, and a quick wit, but he'd just broken up with his fiancée and Dottie had broken up with a guy she'd been dating for two years. So really, they hadn't wanted to see this as anything more than a rebound.

Yet, that day had turned into several, then weeks, and then months. The more he was with her, the more he wanted to be with her...*more*. He didn't have any choice though. He was leaving, and she wasn't interested in being married to a man in the military.

She sighed as they sat at a picnic table and looked out at the forested trail that would lead them back to the parking lot, the road, and civilization. "So you'll be in the military, starting exactly...?"

"I graduate tomorrow and I'll be commissioned. Then I'll attend officer basic training and I'll serve at my first assignment. Not sure where I'll actually be until I'm at my course. What about you?"

"I have another year here before I finish up my degree. Then..." She shrugged. "I'll probably return to Yuma Town, Colorado where I grew up. All my friends still live there."

He knew he didn't have any future with her. Not when he had a five-year military obligation and she was dead set against marrying anyone in the military. She'd been furious with the previous guy she'd been dating for getting a bonus to join up with the navy without even telling her when he planned to just skip out on her. She'd broken up with him right after that.

Jack had even hinted that he would like to see her again when he could take a break. But she hadn't been interested. If her cousin hadn't died in Afghanistan, would she have felt any differently?

Still, he had to flat out ask. "I know this is quick, but, do you want to get married?"

She laughed. "No. If you could get a job in Yuma Town?" She sighed. "Want to run?"

"Yeah, let's do it." He knew he shouldn't have asked her to marry him, that she would say no, but he also knew if he hadn't asked her, he would have been kicking himself over it the whole time he was at the officer's course. He would just have to find someone who was fine with him being in the military. Someone who wasn't going to cheat on him. Someone he cared for like he cared for Dottie.

They stripped, stuffed their clothes in a bag and buried it under brush in the woods where they always hid it, shifted, then ran. He'd miss the time he'd spent with Dottie, and running in the wilderness as a cougar. He hoped he could do so wherever he was while he was in the military. Still, it wouldn't be the same as running with her. Despite knowing he really couldn't make a go of it with her—which was some of the reason she had said she wanted to be with him, just a flash in the pan fun time—he was feeling a hell of a lot more for her than he knew he should.

They'd run for about a mile, watching their surroundings, and he was watching her, when he saw a

3

cougar move nearby in the woods, just a flash of tan fur, but he knew the male. Hellion Crichton—brother to Jack's former fiancée. If Hellion was out here in the woods so close to where they were, Jack suspected it wasn't coincidence. Dottie quickly stopped, watching the other cat, wary like Jack was. The guy didn't have a name like Hellion for nothing. Gigi was close to her brother, but Jack swore the guy was borderline psycho. As soon as the cougar leapt toward Dottie, Jack pounced on him, tearing into him, having to hurt him before Hellion hurt Dottie.

The two cats snarled, clawing at each other, biting, trying to take each other down. Jack wanted Dottie to return to the safety of his SUV, but she stayed there, watching, not getting involved. Which he was glad for. He bit Hellion hard on the leg, trying to break it to disable him enough to get him to quit fighting Jack. Hellion hissed in retaliation and leapt away before Jack could break a bone. Jack hesitated, thinking that Hellion might be ready to give up.

The cougar lunged again. Jack managed to tear at Hellion's neck. Hellion whipped around and bit Jack in the shoulder. Still, Jack was relentless, charging in, biting his opponent twice for every bite Hellion got in. Jack bit Hellion's bad leg again and that seemed to be enough punishment that the cat finally dashed away, his neck bloodied and he was running on three legs. Damn the guy.

Jack must have been a sight too. He was bleeding, though because of their faster healing abilities, he would heal up quickly. Just like Hellion would.

Jack and Dottie loped back to where they'd left their clothes, shifted, and dressed.

"What was that all about?" Dottie growled.

"That was Hellion, my former fiancée's brother. I don't know. Maybe Gigi is angry that I ended the relationship, thinking it was because of you."

"Oh, that's just great."

"Hell, I broke up with Gigi because she's been meeting up with three other guys and having sex with them while she was engaged to me! When I broke up with her, she was furious and said she was a free spirit. Free spirt, my ass. Calling off the engagement has nothing to do with you. We didn't even start dating until several weeks after Gigi and I broke up. Frankly, I didn't believe Gigi cared."

"And you're leaving tomorrow!" Dottie checked over his bite marks on his arms, shoulder, side, and neck. "The claw marks and bite marks aren't deep. You'll live. I'm driving, just in case you pass out though."

The adrenaline flooding his system, Jack felt wired and angry because the cat had gone after Dottie. "I'm not going to pass out."

Dottie narrowed her eyes at him. "You're leaving tomorrow! What if this psycho comes after me when you've left to join the military?"

She was right. What if Hellion did harass her, being the nutcase he was?

"I'm sorry." Jack didn't know what else to say. "I'd eliminate him if I could, just to make sure you'd be safe."

"Then you'd be a wanted criminal? And me a party to it? No thanks."

After half an hour of driving in silence, she parked near his apartment that was three doors down from hers, got out, slammed the door, and stalked off.

He couldn't blame her. Hellion was an ass, but he was also unpredictable. At the same time, Jack hadn't expected the guy to come after him either—or Dottie. And he had no intention of marrying Gigi if she couldn't even be faithful during their engagement. He hadn't been sure how his family would react when he had called it quits with her, but all of them had been glad. When they'd met Dottie, they were hopeful he'd marry her instead. Though he'd told them often enough that she wasn't interested in being an army wife.

At his apartment, he bandaged himself the best he could, called Gigi to tell her what her brother had done to him, thinking as close as she was to him, she could tell him to back off, but she only laughed. Hell, maybe she'd been the one to send her brother after him and Dottie. The thing of it was, Gigi hadn't even been broken up over their canceled engagement. Then again, why would she be? She was already seeing other guys. Angry with him? Yes. In tears at what she'd lost with him? No.

He really wondered if she hadn't cared until she learned *he* was seeing someone else.

After pelting down a couple of beers to numb the pain of his injuries, Jack tried calling Dottie. No answer. He figured she had to cool down. He really hated leaving the situation between them unresolved though.

He felt like hell, the bite wounds burning like crazy. He walked over to her place and knocked on the door. No answer. Not that he expected her to answer the door. Then he noticed her car was gone. He suspected she'd gone to stay with her Aunt Emily. He loved the woman and she was always trying to sway Dottie to marry him. Didn't work though. He thought of running over there, but Dottie had made her point clear. No on marriage. He couldn't get out of his service obligation anyway.

That night when he went to bed, he couldn't quit thinking of Dottie. He had to sleep. Tomorrow after graduation and the commissioning, the movers were coming. He'd stay with his parents that night, and then he was off to his training post. He shut his eyes and all he could see was Dottie's angry expression and it made him feel even worse about having to leave her behind.

***

Dottie packed a bag and headed over to her aunt's house. Hellion had terrified her and no way could she stay at her place if he came over to attack either Jack or her because she was seeing him. Even if Jack was leaving the next day. It didn't mean Hellion knew that.

Every time she became involved with a man, it turned out to be a disaster. She fought going over to see Jack though, to bandage him up. It was hard enough saying goodbye to him. She'd been on the verge of tears every time she thought about him leaving for good. She'd even been in denial about his leaving, trying to pretend the time they had together would go on forever.

This business with Hellion was something else. Jack

should have told her he was leaving her alone with a nest of vipers!

When she arrived at her aunt's house, Aunt Emily tsked. "Jack is the best thing that ever happened to you. You love him, even if you choose to hide behind your cousin's death overseas and your last boyfriend joining the navy without any forewarning." Emily frowned at her. "Did you tell Jack about your dad?"

"No. Why should I?"

"Because that's the other reason you're so adamant about ending this with Jack."

Dottie let out her breath in a huff. "I never think of my dad. Ever. You should have seen the way Hellion came after me when Jack and I were running as cougars in the Ozarks tonight, and then Jack tore into him. I've never seen two cougars fighting. I was in shock. I wanted to leave, but I was afraid Jack might need me. And I was afraid to stay in the event Hellion came after me. I've never been so scared in my life. That's not something anyone ever taught me how to do. Fight, that is."

"So you're not going to Jack's graduation tomorrow?"

Dottie frowned at her aunt. What happened to any sympathy for Hellion coming after them? Her aunt had only

TERRY SPEAR

one thing in mind. Jack was leaving and Dottie should be going with him.

If Dottie went to Jack's graduation, she'd want to see only him, and she'd want to kiss him goodbye and it would break her heart. Best to think of this as a fling like they originally had planned. If she could only forget all the good days and nights they'd had.

"I'm not going." Dottie was ready to move on with her life. Date? No. Just get her degree and return to Yuma Town.

***

The next afternoon after graduation, Jack was finishing up packing his personal items in his Jeep. The movers had loaded the rest of his furniture and boxed goods when Jack saw Hellion headed his way, murder in his black eyes, his neck and arms bandaged where Jack had bitten him. Jack didn't need to get into trouble right before he took off for his training. He wanted to call the police. Unless Hellion threatened him, he couldn't just call them. He had to see what the bastard would say.

Hellion continued to stalk toward him as if no one else existed. The three burly men who were closing up the truck, paused to see what would happen. Jack had his phone out, just in case.

10

Hellion pulled out a 9mm.

Well, hell.

Jack didn't have time to call anyone. He dove for Hellion, taking him down to the sidewalk, and yelled at the other men, "Call the police."

Jack didn't want to have to kill Hellion, just disable him, but he didn't want Hellion to kill any of them either.

"Yeah, a guy armed with a gun is threatening Second Lieutenant Barrington!" The mover quickly gave the address.

Between the hand-to-hand combat training Jack had in AROTC and the karate training he'd taken for years, earning a second-degree black belt, he shoved his hand against Hellion's nose. He heard it crunch just as Hellion fired off a round. The shot went wild and hit Jack's apartment window. A crack sounded behind Jack. *Damn it.* He was glad the round didn't hit him or anyone else though. He threw Hellion to the ground, wrestling with him for the gun. The bastard tried to aim the weapon at Jack.

Jack jumped up and kicked at Hellion's wrist with enough force with his pointed-toe cowboy boot, he heard a bone break in the man's wrist. Hellion howled in pain and lost the gun. If Hellion could have killed Jack right then and there, he would have. Putting one of their kind behind bars could

11

be a real problem if Hellion decided to shift in captivity.

Hellion rolled over on his side and stretched out again for the gun. Sirens wailed in the distance, growing closer as they approached. Jack grabbed Hellion's good arm and flipped him over on his stomach, jerking his arm up against his back to force him to stay or Jack would break his arm.

"Can you kick the gun out of his reach?" Jack shouted to one of the men. He had a damn good hold on Hellion, but he didn't want to risk that the maniac would get loose. God, how he hated that he'd be leaving tomorrow, if he didn't get stuck going to a trial over this, and Dottie could be more at risk.

As soon as three police cars pulled up, the policemen got out of their vehicles and yelled at Jack to get on the ground, their weapons trained at him.

"He's the lieutenant," one of the movers said, motioning between Hellion and the gun. "That's the guy who had the gun and threatened to kill Lieutenant Barrington. It's over there. That guy shot the window instead of one of us because of the lieutenant's quick reaction."

"Hell, this guy is Hellion Crichton," one of the police officers said, taking charge of Hellion. "The store a couple of blocks over caught him on tape when he robbed the quick stop."

That wasn't good—not for being a cougar. Jack hoped If Hellion was found guilty and sentenced to jail, he never shifted while he was incarcerated.

"Hell of a job, lieutenant," one of the policemen said, shaking his hand. "I was in the Air Force."

"Thanks. I'll be on my way to more training tomorrow." Jack gave the police his statement. "Thanks for coming so quickly."

Then the police locked Hellion up in one of the squad cars and took off. Jack imagined the movers had never had so much excitement when moving household goods before. After they wished him luck and headed out, Jack called his apartment manager about the bullet hole in the kitchen window. He was glad Dottie hadn't been here to witness this.

Before he left the next day, he returned to Dottie's apartment one last time, just in case he could see her and say goodbye. Her car wasn't there. He called her aunt. "Oh, my, she said she was going to a friend's graduation ceremony yesterday. I figured it was your graduation ceremony. She didn't see you? She's not here."

He let out his breath, wishing she'd come and congratulated him, or something.

He figured she would return to her apartment once he

was gone. He hated the way they had ended their short-term relationship, despite the fact that neither had expected to have anything more than this.

Yet...he had wanted...more.

.

CHAPTER 1

Nearly five years later

Jack was thrilled to go home for a month to see his family near Branson, Missouri. What he really wanted to do was visit Dottie Hamilton, though he knew she lived in Yuma Town still. Her Aunt Emily did live here and her home was located not far from where his family's home was situated on a lake. He hoped to meet with her and learn what had happened to Dottie the last few years. Aunt Emily had been out of town the last three times he'd been home. Which wasn't often. He hoped Dottie hadn't married and had kids—and was settled in with one big happy family. Well, not that he wouldn't want her to have a happy family. He'd been hopeful that when he finished his service obligation, she'd still be available to renew their relationship.

The problem was he was still in the military, still had a service obligation, and she was completely against being a military wife and having to move all over the country, or overseas. He understood that, never having had a military family or having to move around a lot. Yet, that had been some of the intrigue for him. He had also incurred the service obligation for attending four years of AROTC, most of which he'd worked at long before he met Dottie. Mainly, she hadn't wanted him to get himself killed in some war, leaving her a widow, just like her cousin had done with his wife and three kids.

Jack had only been home for an hour, listening to his mother, Lisa, talk about her garden club and his sister talk about her new boyfriend. Roberta was twenty-seven, like him, his younger twin, and she always had a new boyfriend. He didn't think she'd ever settle down.

Well, him either. In the last nearly five years, he'd dated a lot while he was away in the army. He could never stop thinking about Dottie, his first and only real love. He realized early on he'd lost his heart to her.

"I need to run to the store." He wanted to pick up some things to eat that he liked and drop by and see Aunt Emily.

His mother was browsing through a garden catalogue and looked up at him.

Her blue eyes smiling, Roberta flipped a dark brown curl behind her back. "You're going to see Dottie's aunt. I know. It. You always do. Every time you visit."

"Dottie and I would have been married if—"

"She hadn't said no when you proposed to her. Give it up. You're still in the military, and unless she's changed her mind about being a military wife, you don't stand a chance. Besides, by now, she's probably married and raising a passel of cougar babies, and not waiting for you to come around."

He let his breath out in exasperation. Roberta had never felt anything for a guy like he did about Dottie. She couldn't understand.

"I'll see you all later."

"Coming home for lunch?" his mother asked.

"Nah. I'll just grab something while I'm out. I might run by Royce's house and see how he's doing. Play some video games for a while. I'll be back later." Jack loved seeing his family, but he found visiting to be tedious after a few hours. No one wanted to hear about his job. He wasn't interested in his mom's prize irises, or Roberta's string of boyfriends. When his dad returned home after dealing with computer

17

support issues all day, he would talk with him. They actually both loved playing computer games, fishing, boating, and camping. So he'd always been close to his dad.

Before he went anywhere, he called Aunt Emily, hoping she was in good health, was here this time, and free to see him.

"Omigod, yes, come right over. Can you come right over?" Emily was so excited about hearing from him, she cheered him up right away. She'd always wanted Dottie to marry him, so maybe this was good news. Dottie must still be available. At least he hoped that was the reason for Emily's enthusiasm.

"I'll be right over." Within twenty minutes, he was parking in the driveway of the little white French provincial style home, a white picket fence out front, red roses and red crepe myrtles all along the border. Her place was on the other side of the lake from where his parents lived. Emily didn't even wait for him to get to the front brick walk before she was heading out to see him as if he were her long, lost son. He loved her, her dark brown hair graying at the temples, her smile contagious.

"You are a sight for sore eyes." She gave him a big hug and took his hand to lead him inside. "If I'd had more warning, I would have baked your favorite blueberry muffins. No matter, I'll do it now."

He laughed. "I didn't come over here to make you work."

"Oh, I know. You came over to see me because you love me." She smiled up at him. "And you love Dottie." She shook her head. "I don't know what's the matter with my niece. She is so pig-headed about you being in the military. If I had been her, I would have married you in a heartbeat and even been fighting beside you in the field, protecting your back."

"You've always been my favorite aunt."

She laughed. "You don't have one."

"Sure I do. I adopted you the day I met you."

They walked inside her comfortable home, and she led him into the kitchen. "Have you been in touch with her?"

"I tried a few times after I left. She didn't reply. She had already told me she wasn't interested. I know she was close to her cousin, and that affected the way she felt about the military."

Aunt Emily sighed. "We all loved Buddy. That's not a good enough reason to give you up. You're the best thing that's ever happened to her." She began making up the batter for the muffins. "Okay, listen. She might not have ever told you about her father. He'd also been in the military."

Jack couldn't believe it. "Don't tell me he died in a conflict too."

"Not a military conflict. He had an unaccompanied tour overseas, no family allowed to stay with him, except for short visits for the nine months he was over there. He hooked up with a woman—a married woman. When her husband discovered the adulterous affair, he killed both of them."

"Hell."

"Yeah. That's another reason Dottie is so afraid of being a military wife. That her husband would have to go off on assignment and might pick up another woman. Even though it can happen in any line of business, or at home even. Still, her mother was affected horribly by it, and that affected Dottie. She was five at the time. Then her mother and Chase Buchanan's parents were at a New Year's party a year later, heading home. Their car hit ice and went into the river. The coroner pronounced them dead at the scene. Dottie lived with me then, taking trips back to Yuma Town to see her friends."

"She didn't reveal any of that to me. Whenever I tried to talk to her about her parents, she just said they'd died."

"You can imagine it still is a sore subject for her. So how

long are you going to be here this time?"

"A month. I just arrived a couple of hours ago."

Aunt Emily stirred the blueberry muffin batter while Jack sat at the bar and watched. "That's great news! I wish I could say Dottie was visiting around the same time as you. She hasn't been here in a good long while." Emily looked up from the bowl of batter. "She's not married, but she's been married."

The way her aunt looked at him, frowning, he suspected it hadn't been a good marriage. It sounded like they were no longer married either. So that was good news.

"He'd been in the military like you."

That revelation had Jack's ire stoked. She couldn't marry him, but she could marry some other guy who was in the military? Maybe she really hadn't felt anything for him after all.

"He'd already left the military when he met her, and he'd kept his past secret from her. She didn't even know he'd been in," Emily quickly said. "It was a strange situation. She left here, went back to Yuma Town, and I don't know, within the month, she married him. She said very little about him, just that he was making lots of money as a computer software salesman, and I was concerned that meeting him

21

and marrying him was so sudden. She said she'd known him for some time before that. So I figured he was a college student. He wasn't. I thought she must have met him in Yuma Town, and she had. I only learned much later that he wasn't from there either."

"Okay so you said they're no longer married. How long have they been divorced?"

"He's dead. Another cougar killed him to protect her and the..." Emily paused.

"Kids? She has kids? By him?" That changed everything. Jack realized she really wasn't the same woman he'd known when they had attended college. She was no longer a never-been married, single cougar. She was a mother with...how many kids? Then he remembered the part about the guy being dead and that she'd needed protection from him. *Hell.* Jack would have taken the bastard out, and protected both her and the kids.

"Yeah. An adorable little boy and girl. You know, if I didn't know better"—Emily paused to fill the muffin tins with batter—"I'd say they were yours. Just guessing. You know, the timing would have been right. Much more right than if her ex-husband had been the babies' father. She didn't meet him until well after you were gone. And she had the babies nine months after you left."

Completely blind-sighted, Jack's jaw dropped, and he stared at Emily as if she'd told him she knew he was a purple-horned unicorn—and she believed it.

***

Dottie Brown had been meaning to see her aunt and just that morning had been thinking about making the trip when Aunt Emily gave her a call at the Yuma Town sheriff's department where Dottie was a dispatcher. She figured it was a good reminder to see her.

"Hey, I'm not getting any younger, you know. I haven't seen the kids since they were babies. They're four now, and old enough to ride some of the kiddy rides at the theme park. Why don't you ask that boss of yours to give you some time off to see me? You know I'm terrified of flying and it's too far for me to drive."

"I wish you'd just move up here to Yuma Town and live with me or at least nearby."

"I have too many friends here, and I have to visit your Uncle Jeff's grave and my son's once a week. I couldn't bear to leave them. We'll have fun. We always do. Even if you don't want to see me, I've been dying to see my grand-niece and nephew. They're all I have, you know. With Buddy gone, that was the end of me having any chance to have grandchildren."

"Of course I want to see you. Honestly? I've been thinking about it a lot lately."

"Don't just think about it. Tell me you'll come. I'll pay for your airfare even."

"You don't have—"

"I want to. Just confirm with your boss that you can take the time off, and we'll have a load of fun."

Dottie was excited about the prospect of seeing her aunt, and the kids getting to know her better. "I'll give you a call right back."

"Make it by Wednesday, will you? The weather's perfect, and I don't want to put this off any longer. You might change your mind."

Dottie smiled. "I won't change my mind. That's only two days from now. I'll have to see if the sheriff's department can get another dispatcher to cover for me."

"For two and a half weeks."

"That's kind of a long time. They might think I'm not coming back."

"The Renaissance festival starts in another week, and I'll get the kids' costumes for it. They can use them for

Halloween then. You never visit me. Please, come for a couple of weeks at least."

"All right, all right." How could Dottie say no when her aunt did love children. Dottie could really use a break and a change of setting for some plain old fun with the kids. It would be entertaining for all of them. "I'll call you in a little while."

As soon as she was on the phone to Dan, he gave her a hard time, teasing in his way. "We'll never be able to manage without you."

"Okay, so, just a week?"

"No way. You take the two and a half weeks. Three if you need them. We'll be fine. You need to visit your aunt, and let her see Trish and Jeff before they're all grown up. Time doesn't sit still for anyone."

"All right. If you get in a bind because I'm gone—"

"We'll handle it. Stryker can drive you and the kids to the airport."

"Wednesday is fine with you then?"

"Sure. And have fun. No thinking about work. Just enjoy your visit with your family."

She never knew what was going on with Dan. He loved her kids and was good to her. Still, he was holding back concerning any real relationship with her. She thought she could live that way, just enjoying his company when they could both get together. She realized she really wanted more. She wanted a father for her children. A live-in daddy. A loving husband. A mate.

She was trying not to think about Jack's service obligation and that it was nearly up, though she couldn't help it. She'd never cared for another man like she did him. But so much time had passed, and so much had happened, she knew they were two very different people now.

She'd heard another Cougar Special Forces Division agent, who handled cougar-related issues, was coming into Yuma Town. She wondered if maybe he might be someone she could be interested in. The problem with Dan was they'd been friends since they were kids. She thought that might be the reason he was pulling away.

She sighed and called her aunt back. "Okay, Wednesday it is. Just let me know the flight times and we'll be on our way down there in a couple of days."

"Oh, I'm so thrilled. We'll have so much fun. I'll send it to you in just a minute. Bye, honey. Love you."

"Love you too."

Within minutes Dottie had the itinerary in her email. Her

aunt had scheduled her for a flight at six Wednesday morning? Ugh. Didn't her aunt remember Dottie had two little kids to take to the airport?

She hoped they didn't miss their flight.

***

Emily gave Jack a thumbs up. "She's coming. Now don't you dare fight with her when they get here. I want her to visit with me, not return home right away."

Jack couldn't believe Emily had managed to pull this off. He was thrilled.

"No mentioning the kids might be yours. There's time enough for that later. She's had to adjust to a lot of major changes in her life since you saw her last. She's not the same person at all. Having the twins, a failed marriage, nearly losing her house, reinventing herself with her new job as a police dispatcher, and the ex coming back to threaten her has changed her."

He didn't care. He realized some time ago that he loved her and had always loved her. "Has she been seeing anyone since the ex was out of her life?" He worried that she might already have someone new she was seeing and that being away in the army for three and a half more months could mean he'd lose out. Not that he could do anything about the time he had left in the service.

"She's been seeing a few guys. Nothing in the least bit serious. Not everyone wants to marry a woman, or a man, and then have to help raise someone else's kids. The thing of it is though, she's fine on her own. She supports herself. So she really doesn't need anyone else in her life right now. Just remember that. You have two and a half weeks to convince her she wants you no matter what else is holding her back from marrying you." Emily shrugged. "Though the two of you might not care for each other after all of this time. Which would be a crying shame. In which case, I get to see my adorable grand-niece and nephew anyway. If she does want to go out with you, I'll be the perfect babysitter for the kids." She tilted her head in question. "What about this business with the army? Do you plan to make it a career?"

"I have three and a half more months left on my service obligation. If she's not interested, I'll stay in. I know it's hard to have a long-distance relationship that works. If she feels anything for me like I feel for her, I want to give it a shot. If she wants to make a go of it, then maybe we can make it happen this time." He didn't know what else he would work at if he left the army. Would she still want to live in Yuma Town? He figured he wouldn't be able to get a computer science type job there. He'd only ever thought about staying with the military. And being with Dottie. He couldn't believe she had kids that could be his and she hadn't told him about them. Then again, he could. He was certain she would have worried that he'd want partial custody to take them away from her so he had time to get to know them, if she wasn't interested in being with him. "Is she still in Yuma Town?"

All he knew was that if they were his kids, he wanted to be part of their lives too.

"Yeah. After you left, she ended up returning to Yuma Town, met Jeffrey Brown, married him, divorced him, and she hasn't left. She loves it there and has lots of close friends. Like I have close friends here. I'm not sure that she'd want to move the kids to somewhere else. It's a great cougar community, from what she's told me. Out here? Not so much. I mean, it's perfect to run in the wilderness as cougars, but it's nice having a bunch of cougars to help out. Especially when you have kids. There are other cougar kids to play with and she's had a lot of help with taking care of them while she's had to work."

If they could get their relationship back on track, he'd be thrilled if he could provide her enough support that she could stay home with the kids. As long as that's what she wanted.

"The guy's name was Jeffrey?"

"Yeah. She thought one of the reasons she liked her husband was because of his name. She adored her Uncle Jeff. I guess she thought this guy would be nice like him, and he probably treated her well while they dated. I met him once. He didn't care for me. I think it was because I could see clean through him. That he was hiding who he really was from her. I really believe she felt pressured to marry because she was pregnant, and hopeful that it would work out. I shouldn't be telling you this, but her son's middle name is Alexander."

Jack smiled. "She only called me that when she was mad at me."

Emily smiled and patted him on the chest. "Make her fall in love with you. Be your charming self with her like you are with me. And don't, whatever you do, screw this up. I know I said she doesn't need anyone in her life. I know, for me, if I had you in my life, I'd be all set."

That was one hell of a tall order if Dottie didn't even want to see Jack when she arrived at the airport Wednesday afternoon. He couldn't wait to see her and the kids too.

"Do you want me to pick her up?" He wanted to. He wanted to see her right away. He only had two and a half weeks to make this happen.

"She'd probably feel she was hoodwinked into coming here. But yeah, we might as well show her we mean business." She washed her hands. "And don't mention her ex-husband. That's a sore subject!"

"Do you have pictures of the twins?"

"Oh, of course. Tons of them." Emily wiped her hands on the kitchen towel. "I'll be right back."

As soon as she returned with a photo album full of pictures and started showing them to him, he smiled. "Hell, Jeff looks just like me when I was that age. And Trish has Dottie's smile."

"That's what I was thinking. Well, I haven't seen your pictures as a child. I could still see your expression when he's concentrating on something, or laughing."

Hell, Jack wasn't going to sleep a wink until he saw her again. Two kids? Twins? He was sure they were his. He hadn't foreseen that coming. It was all the more reason to convince her this could work out between them. He sure hoped they could make it work.

CHAPTER 2

Dottie was excited about seeing her aunt, getting away from work, and taking her kids to the Renaissance fair and theme park. Trish and Jeff were too. They were so tired after she had to get them up so early, they fell asleep on the plane right away.

She knew the kids would love her aunt, just as much as she did. Emily had always made things fun for her while she was growing up. A fun-filled adventure. The twins hadn't stopped talking about the trip, except getting them up this morning had been a different story. She hadn't stopped thinking about the vacation either, and was just as excited to be going home for a visit.

Emily had even bought them first class tickets so they'd have the royal treatment. Jeff and Trish had worn their pint-sized cowboy hats and worn western boots, just like they always did.

When they finally arrived at the airport, Trish and Jeff pulled their own wheeled, pint-sized luggage. Jeff's was covered in horses and cowboys; Trish's in ballerinas in purple tutus. They were already hungry, and still a little sleepy, as they made their way to the elevator so they could reach the baggage claim at the lower level. Dottie expected Emily to be waiting down there. What she didn't expect was to see her old boyfriend, Jack Barrington, holding up a sign that said: VIP Dottie Hamilton and Kids, Adventure Tours of a Lifetime!

Completely shocked, she stopped dead in her tracks, raised her brows at seeing Jack standing there, still referring to her maiden name on the sign, like anyone in town would who knew her by her maiden name. If Jack was here, and he obviously already knew she had kids, he had to know that Hamilton was no longer her name and her dear, sweet Aunt Emily had set this whole thing up.

She tried not to feel the quiver in her belly, or the headiness she felt at seeing him. It was like she was single again, in college, and seeing him for the first time. He was smiling a little, a dimple showing in one cheek, his blue eyes twinkling with merriment. He appeared excited to see her, but was waiting also to see her reaction to his being here.

She took a steadying breath and walked toward him, her legs a little wobbly, knowing now why her aunt had been so insistent that Dottie come right this minute and not delay. Most likely because Jack had a plane to catch soon, to whatever army assignment he had now. She couldn't believe her aunt had orchestrated this whole thing without letting her know what she was up to. Then again, Aunt Emily had always wanted her to marry him. Which meant, he had to be single, at the least. Did he have kids? An ex?

Jack's smile broadened, and that warm and generous smile made her heartbeat thump even harder. He smiled at the kids too, like he really liked kids. And in that instant, she saw Jeff's expression reflected in Jack's.

She suspected Emily told him to put on his best showmanship if he was going to win her over. She hadn't changed her mind about wanting to be a military wife and being dragged all over the world and back. If he was thinking of settling down...maybe they had a chance with each other.

Now, more than ever, she needed a safe place for her kids to grow up. So she didn't want to leave the safety of Yuma Town. She hadn't changed her mind about him either—at least not from a physical standpoint. He was as gorgeous as ever—tanned, muscled, and beautiful.

And her first and only genuine love. The guy she'd been dating before she met Jack hadn't even compared.

So much had happened since they were in college together and there was no going back to those carefree days. She imagined he'd changed too after all the war experiences he'd had over the past five years.

"Kids, this is Jack Barrington. A good friend of mine when I went to college here. Jack, this is Trish, and Jeff."

"What a lovely name," Jack said, crouching to get to eye level with her and offering his hand to shake hers. After shaking her hand, he turned to Jeff. "And this wrangler is Jeff?"

Jeff stuck out his hand like all the guys taught him to greet a stranger or a friend with a good, sturdy handshake, though for four years old, he still didn't have a really good grip.

Jack laughed. "That's a mighty fine handshake, young man."

Jeff beamed at him.

Jack rose to his feet and leaned over to give Dottie a kiss on the cheek, sweet, a getting-to-know-you-all-over kiss. She fought throwing her arms around him and giving him a kiss that said she wanted more with him.

"I take it you're here on leave for two and a half weeks?" she asked, hoping he was and that was the reason Emily had wanted them to stay as long as that.

"A month, actually. Emily was afraid asking you to come any longer than two and a half weeks was pushing it."

Dottie let out her breath and shook her head. "I was married, so I no longer use my maiden name, Hamilton."

"You will always be a Hamilton to me, Dottie. That's all Aunt Emily calls you too, you know."

She still couldn't believe how sneaky her aunt had been. What else was Emily hoping to do to get them back together? "So where *is* Aunt Emily?"

"She was going to come. She was afraid to leave the turkey in the oven cooking if she came to the airport. She's in the middle of preparing a big feast for you, just like it was Christmas. She has been so excited about seeing you and the kids."

Dottie smiled. That sounded like her aunt. The last time she visited when the babies were just a year old, her aunt had made it feel like Christmas then too. "What are you doing here?"

"I have a month of vacation saved up and promised to

see my family. Of course, anytime I come here, I try to see your aunt."

"So you're still in the army." She was hoping he could take an early release from the army, if there was any such thing. "Not that I'm surprised. I kind of was keeping track of the approximate time when you'd be getting out, if you got out." She probably shouldn't have mentioned that part, giving him the notion she'd been thinking about him a lot and counting the days until he was free of the army, even if she had been.

His mouth curved up again as he took her carry-on bags and offered to take the kids' too. They loved pulling them just like adults, so they hung onto their handles and shook their heads. "Yep. I have another three and a half month's service obligation back at Fort Hood. After that? We'll see."

He held the door open for the elevator and gave her a look like he knew she felt something for him, like he did for her.

"I thought you had always wanted to make a career of it."

"If I had no better offer."

After riding in the elevator, they reached the luggage carousal. Trish said she needed to go to the bathroom.

"Do you need to go?" Dottie asked her son.

He shook his head.

"He can stay with me and help look for the bags."

"Are you sure?"

"Yeah, we'll be fine."

"Okay, thanks." She took Trish to the bathroom, surprised Jack wasn't turned off by kids. He'd never really talked about having any. Of course, they'd never really gotten that far in their relationship either. Then again, if he was here, knowing she had them, that was an indication he was willing to see how this played out. She imagined it would be a big shock to him as far as dealing with kids went. Then she wondered, had her aunt believed the kids were his? Had she told him? She ground her teeth.

She really wished his service obligation was over. She understood how he'd just continue on with his army career, if they couldn't make a connection in the next couple of weeks.

When she and Trish were done at the restroom, they headed back to join Jack and her son.

The bags were going around on the carousal now and Jeff had pointed out several that looked like theirs. Jack smiled when he saw her coming with Trish, holding her hand.

"Didn't find them yet?" Dottie asked.

"They all look alike."

"There's one!" Dottie said, and immediately Jack hurried forth to get the bag. For the most part, she was used to doing everything for herself, so she appreciated the help. "And that one."

"So, you disappeared and I couldn't say goodbye," he said, hauling the bags to them.

She'd felt bad that she hadn't bandaged his wounds that day. She had just been angry that Jack hadn't told her how volatile Hellion was, though she suspected afterward he hadn't known either. And she'd been scared that Hellion would come after her next once Jack was long gone.

"I went to your graduation ceremony, and watched you raise your hand to take the oath to serve in the military." In his uniform, he'd been so dashing, and she'd cried then, wishing she hadn't felt the way she had about him going into the service. It was a good thing she hadn't joined him when she learned she was having twins. She couldn't imagine living in post housing and dealing with being a cougar shifter with twins. "I closed up my apartment, lived with Aunt Emily for a short while, then returned home."

"Why didn't you come to see me?" Then he dropped the

subject. "You didn't finish your degree?"

She shook her head, and rubbed Jeff's back, a silent statement that said she'd had to deal with more important business—like being single and pregnant with cougar shifter babies on the way. "I returned to Yuma Town and met Jeffrey when he was passing through. I didn't want to worry about Hellion coming after me. I was afraid that if I stayed and he learned I was pregnant..."

"He might have assumed the babies were mine." Jack studied her for a moment and she was certain he realized then, if he didn't know before, the kids *were* his. "I understand completely. Hellion came after me the next day, armed with a gun."

Her jaw dropped.

"I took him down and the police arrested him. Luckily, the movers were there and witnessed the whole situation. I had friends who kept an eye on him, just in case he ever tried to come after you, until he went to jail. He had robbed a quick stop before he came to see me. He's been in jail the last five years—theft, aggravated assault, armed robbery, though he plea bargained and he received a reduced sentence. From what I understand, he's had no issues with his shifting at the jailhouse, thankfully. I was glad you'd left that day, or you might have been involved in the altercation. He shot a bullet through my apartment window even."

"I...I didn't know. I haven't been here in quite a while. I really thought my aunt wanted to see me and the kids," she said as he carried her bags to his Jeep. She was glad Jack hadn't mentioned the issue of the kids. She needed to talk to him first about it before she said anything to Jeff and Trish. "I never expected her to be so sneaky."

Jack smiled. "I came over to visit her and as soon as she learned I was going to be here a while, she called you up, thinking this was the right time for your visit. She can't wait to see you and the kids. She just had an added incentive to encourage you to come, right this minute."

"I swear if she wasn't your mother's age, she'd marry you on the spot."

He laughed. "I don't have an aunt, so I adopted her. I always visit her when I return to see my family. She never told me you had married or had kids."

Dottie had forgotten how close he was to his family and would be visiting them periodically. She appreciated that. That was one of the reasons she liked him. Family meant everything to her. Even her friends back in Yuma Town that were like family to her.

"I imagine she didn't want to chase you off in the event you still might leave the service and get back together with me."

"I agree. Aunt Emily said you might be tired and after the feast, everyone can lie down. I want to return and take you to the movies tonight."

"With the kids?" She didn't mean to sound so surprised. She just hadn't envisioned him jumping in to do things with her and the kids too.

"Sure and with Aunt Emily."

She smiled at him. "This isn't a devious way to get my aunt out on a date, is it?"

He laughed. "We'll all have fun."

***

Jack had enjoyed the feast with Aunt Emily, Dottie, and the kids, as if they were sitting down to a Thanksgiving dinner. Then he let them rest and returned later to pick them up to take them to the movies. Aunt Emily had eagerly asked if they wanted her to take the kids to see an animated feature while Jack and Dottie saw something else.

Jack wanted to see the animated film with the family. If he was going to learn how to be a daddy, this was the only way to go. If any of his army buddies had asked him what he was going to do when he arrived home, this would have been the furthest thing from his mind.

He was certain that Dottie hadn't made the slip about being pregnant before she left town and that's why she hadn't finished college, plus the concern about Hellion. He assumed she wanted to talk to him about the kids when they were alone.

"Let's all go together." He wondered then if Dottie would tell the kids that he was really their father. Maybe it would be too confusing if she decided she didn't want to marry him. If he *was* their father, he did want to tell them when she thought it would be the best time for it.

At the movie, he had a blast with the kids. He had his arm around Dottie the whole time as if they were on a date, because as far as he was concerned they were and every hour counted. Even if they had two kids and her aunt on the date. The kids were really cute, fascinated with the animated feature, watching it as if everything that was happening was real. He'd forgotten what being that young was like.

They'd had popcorn and sodas and hotdogs even. And after they put Trish and Jeff to bed that night, Aunt Emily said, "Go. Run. I'll undress the kids so you can shift and they can sleep as cougar cubs until you return."

He didn't wait for Dottie to agree. "Do you have a spare room for me to change in?"

"You don't have to be all modest for me," her aunt said.

The way Dottie's cheeks blushed, he figured her aunt had embarrassed her. He was used to her aunt joking with him like that though.

He smiled and went to the room Emily pointed out. He wouldn't ever forget the last time he'd gone running with Dottie as cougars and the trouble that had led to. With Hellion in jail, it shouldn't be an issue this time. Jack wanted to run with the kids too while they were visiting. That should be a real experience and a half. He couldn't wait.

***

That night with the full moon shining down on the shadowy woods, Jack had a lovely time running through the trees, stopping with Dottie to drink from a pond, and enjoying each other's company. He was trying not to think about the kids, or how much they looked like him. Or how much he was certain they were his. What if she'd been with another guy after he'd left and they really hadn't been his? That her aunt and he had it all wrong? Yet, he thought the kids looked too much like him to believe someone else was the father.

He was having a hard time refraining from bringing up the issue about the ex-husband also, wondering exactly what had happened concerning him—how, when, and why he was killed. Aunt Emily didn't know the details, and she had reminded him not to mention it to Dottie unless he wanted to create problems between them. If Dottie wanted to bring up the subject at this point, it was up to her.

He was trying to envision being with Dottie as a husband and father, something he'd never anticipated. A husband, yes. Not both all at once. He'd imagined in a few years after they were married, they'd have a couple of kids, if it ever came to that. Nothing like coming home to four-year-old twins.

So why hadn't she told him? Because she thought he'd insist they get married, and she didn't want to be an army wife? Or maybe she was worried they couldn't resolve where they were going to live and she was afraid he'd want custody.

He was already thinking of cutting his vacation short, just leave it at two and a half weeks so he could visit with Dottie, the kids, and her aunt for the whole time, then return to his post and take the one and half weeks of accumulated leave at the end of his obligation, so he could get out earlier.

After they returned to the house, they shifted and

dressed. Dottie dressed the kids in their pajamas, and then he and she went outside to sit on the porch swing.

"I'm not staying in the army." He'd decided already. If he was going to make it work between them, he had to do whatever he could. Two and a half weeks weren't enough time, not with another three month separation to get through. Maybe she wouldn't ever want to mate him, but he wanted to be there for the kids. His kids. If they truly were his. And maybe she'd eventually change her mind about him too. Surely, he could find some kind of job in Yuma Town.

"You said you had another three and a half months left of your service obligation."

"I do. What I'm going to do is stay here for only the amount of time you'll be here, saving up one and a half weeks of my vacation time to take at the end of the three months. That way I can see you sooner. Then again, you and the kids can see me anytime while I'm still stationed at Fort Hood."

She folded her arms as he rested his arm around her shoulders. "So you get out of the army and then what? You don't think I'm going to support you, do you?"

He knew she was teasing. He'd been working since he was thirteen. He couldn't imagine not working at something. "I've never been to Yuma Town. Is there anything there that

I could work at?"

She shook her head. "We haven't seen each other in five years. One night at the movies isn't going to make all the difference in the world."

"We have the theme park, runs with the kids in the woods, visits to the ice cream shop, the zoo, the Renaissance fair, just all kinds of adventures. By then, I'll have worn you down and you'll realize what a great guy I am. Again."

She laughed, then raised a brow. "No dinners out with just you?"

"Hell yeah."

She smiled. "Okay. I thought you were just trying for father of the year."

"About that." Jack had to know if the kids were his. No way could he pretend they weren't, if they were, and he wanted the kids and her in his life, support-wise, and every other way. Even, he realized, if they weren't his. He couldn't imagine not having a father figure in his life. They needed one too.

She looked away. "I wondered when you'd ask. Yes, I was married to a man named Jeffrey Brown, though that wasn't his real name. He was prior military and I later learned during one of the engagements he was in, he tried to kill a fellow serviceman, Leyton Hill, who now lives in Yuma Town and is the field director working for the CSFD."

Jack thought Dottie was going to talk to him about the kids, so he was surprised when she mentioned the loser of an ex-husband instead. He was glad to learn about him though too. "The CSFD?" He'd never heard of them before.

"The Cougar Special Forces Division. They deal with rogue cougars."

"In Yuma Town?" He thought that the place was supposed to be safe for the kids and her.

"Yeah, but they don't stay around there. They take off to other locations, wherever they're needed to take down the rogues."

Which gave Jack a great idea. Surely, if they had any openings, he could get on with them. He was prior service, like Leyton, and combat-trained.

"So what happened? Aunt Emily said your ex-husband was killed when he had threatened you." He wished he'd been there for Dottie, though he couldn't have gotten out of his service obligation for anything.

"Leyton killed him. Though his mate had a hand in it. Jeffrey had already injured another CSF agent named Travis, who also lives in Yuma Town. Well, he'd tried to kill Leyton too." She let out her breath. "I know what you're thinking—about the kids. Jeff and Trish are yours."

Dottie couldn't have hit him squarer in the jaw with the comment than she did. He thought they were. This confirmed it and he thought he'd be prepared for the truth. He wasn't. He was glad to hear it, but afraid she wouldn't want him in her life for good.

"They are," he said, matter-of-factly. They looked just like him, except their hair was blonder than his was. Then again, his was just as light when he was that young. It had darkened the older he got. Dottie and her aunt were dark-haired like her father and his father.

"Yes. I didn't plan to keep it a secret from you. As soon as I saw you at the airport, I wanted to tell you. I just couldn't mention it in front of the kids. What if you'd fainted?"

He laughed. He loved her sense of humor. "I'm not the fainting type. Though if you told me we'd had sextuplets, then maybe. You know what this means, don't you?"

"We're not getting married. Not just so the kids will have a mother and father who live together. The kids never knew Jeffrey. He left when they were a year old. He said he was going on a job and I kept thinking he would return any day, but he never came back. I finally filed for divorce. I was going to lose the house, and my friend Dan Steinecker, the sheriff, my boss, and a good friend came out and talked with me. His dispatcher wanted to retire and I took her place. Initially, Jeffrey had wanted me to say the kids were his. It was a condition of the marriage. When I look back at the situation, I believe he used me and the kids as a cover for his illegal operations. Then he took off to do more of his illicit business and didn't return until much later when Leyton had to take him out. I divorced him by default. He never responded when I filed for divorce. Dan hired a PI he knows to locate Jeffrey and serve him the papers. I was glad he wasn't dead, and he had a chance to respond, though I was afraid of what he might say about the kids, custody rights, visitation rights, that sort of thing."

"Great father figure."

She cast Jack a dark look.

"Just saying." Why hadn't she contacted Jack? "Okay, so yeah, we need to get to know each other again. They're my kids too. I've always been close to my dad. I want that for Trish and Jeff also."

"You are still in the army."

"For three and a half more months. Three," he corrected.

"A lot can happen in that time. You could find someone else."

Jack snorted. "I haven't found anyone else in all the time we've been apart. All I've ever thought about is you. Anyone I've ever dated couldn't hold a candle to you. The only real problem we had was my being in the army, and I couldn't do anything about that."

"Why don't we see what happens after you get out, *if* you get out."

"I'll be sending support money home to you for you and the kids."

"For the kids, if you want. It's not necessary. I make enough on my own to support them."

He wasn't going to repeat that the kids were his too, and he had a financial obligation to help support them. More than that? He wanted to do all the things he had done with his father with his own kids. And Dottie too, if she wanted to go with them. As a family. He'd never considered he'd end up with a readymade family. It would take some adjusting for everyone. He suspected the only one who wouldn't have to adjust to the notion was Aunt Emily.

"I need to go to bed. The kids will be up early, and I don't want to impose on my aunt to have to take care of them first thing in the morning."

He rose from the swing and took Dottie's hand and pulled her into his arms. "I want this to be the beginning for us."

"You. Are. Leaving. Again. For three more months."

"I'll be back. In the meantime, I want to keep in touch, emails, Skype, phone calls. And you and the kids can visit me. I want you to know I'm not out of your lives, and before you know it, I'll be back."

"Without a job."

He smiled. "I won't move in so you can support me."

"I'm not leaving Yuma Town and I'm not leaving my job as a police dispatcher. I love it there."

"No problem at all." Though he wondered what kind of reception he'd get in Yuma since he hadn't ever supported his own kids. Even though he hadn't known about them. He imagined they were a tight-knit community since they were mostly cougar shifters.

He kissed her then, just like he had in the past, full of passion and loving. She responded just as heartily as if she was ready to renew this business between them, despite sounding like she didn't think it would work out. He guessed she'd been so disappointed with relationships in the past, she couldn't see that with him she might have a real future. He wished he didn't have to return to his army job for any length of time at all.

***

Dottie threw herself into the kiss with enthusiasm, as if she and Jack had never been apart. She realized then, just how much she'd missed Jack. How much this felt right between them. It was as if all the years they'd been apart just melted away, and he was the same person she knew before the marriage, the divorce, and the kids.

She wanted this. She hadn't been sure of it when she'd first seen him. When he first kissed her sweetly in front of her kids. Their kids. This passion that always exploded between them—this was what she was missing in her life.

She wrapped her arms around him and listened to his heart beating as rapidly as hers, breathed in his spicy scent that was all his, and wished he was free to come home with her, right this very minute. For now, she wouldn't let him go and was just enjoying the feel of his hard, hot body pressed against her, the way he kept his arms tightly around her as if he was experiencing the same thing.

"I've missed this with you," she told him honestly.

"Hell, I didn't realize just how much I truly missed you

until I saw you at the airport and wanted to kiss you like this. Before that, it was just a case of remembering how good it was between us until Hellion got involved."

"Thanks for making sure that someone was keeping an eye on him until he went to jail."

"Yeah, he certainly deserved it."

She let out her breath on a heady sigh. "I guess we'd better call it a night so we can get up early to go to the theme park."

He kissed her forehead. "Okay, sounds good." He gave her another kiss on the mouth, and then he left, and she wished he could have stayed.

She was so glad her aunt had been the master manipulator and had gotten them back together, helping her to share with him about his kids—though she had been unsure how he would react.

She couldn't wait to see how things went at the theme park tomorrow. She hoped if the kids grew cranky, Jack could deal with it in a good way. Not all men could handle being around kids when children were at their worst. And Jack hadn't had any experience with any of this, good or bad.

***

When Jack went home that night, he was full of hope

that things would work out between him and Dottie, and that this wasn't all some crazy notion he had that the kids would love him and she would too. It was one thing to pay child support, another to really raise a family. And to marry the woman he'd fallen hard for so long ago.

His mother, father, and sister were sitting in the living room, waiting for him to come home. He knew it all had to do with him and Dottie, though he didn't really want to discuss this with the family right this minute.

His sister spoke first. "Okay, so did she tell you they were your kids?"

"You knew? Let me get a beer." He couldn't believe his sister had known all along and had never told him.

His mom was sitting on the edge of her seat, anxious for the news. His dad was just smiling at him like he was amused that Jack had come home to learn he had a family. His sister appeared eager to clear the air. Just how much had she known? Had everyone else also?

Beer in hand, Jack sat on one of the chairs. "Okay, so, yes, Trish and Jeff are my kids."

His mother burst into tears.

CHAPTER 3

"Did you tell him?" Aunt Emily asked Dottie as she came in for the night, ready to go to bed.

"Yeah. He would have known. Like you knew, right?" Dottie hadn't thought anyone had. She had guessed wrong.

"Yeah. I'm glad you let him in on the truth. He needed to know."

Dottie told her what they had talked about.

"Then there's hope the two of you will get together for good in three months."

"Three months is still a long time."

"Dottie Susan May Hamilton, you wait it out. No seeing other guys. The kids are Jack's. Give him a chance to be part of the family. It's nearly been five years. Give him three more months. It won't kill you."

Dottie rarely heard her aunt's voice raised in annoyance. "Okay, okay." She was anyway; she was just afraid to be let down.

"Are you going to tell the kids?"

"I think we need to wait—"

"Okay, listen. Let's say you don't get together. He's going to support the kids. He'll want to see them. He's their father. So you need to tell them. Even if it doesn't work out between you. It's not his fault that he didn't know he had a couple of kids. He knows now. It's time you told everyone the truth."

That was not going to be easy. "I agree. I will. Night, Aunt Emily." Dottie had thought she was going to come home to see her aunt and her aunt would enjoy seeing the kids and that was it. She'd never expected all of this to happen.

As soon as she was ready for bed and pulled her covers over her shoulder, her phone rang. Instinctively, she knew it had to be Jack, unless someone in Yuma Town needed to get hold of her about something. She doubted it. She checked the caller ID. *Jack.* Now what? "Hello?"

"Well, I walked into an interrogation room when I arrived home."

She smiled. Poor Jack. "So your family knew about the

kids too?"

"They suspected. My sister said she knew for sure. Anyway, my mother burst into tears, hit me, hugged me, and wants to see the kids as soon as you're okay with it."

Dottie sighed. "This was just supposed to be a vacation."

"Can they see the kids?"

"Of course. My aunt will be delighted. I'm not sure how the kids are going to take all of this. Would your family be interested in going to the theme park with us? Or the Renaissance fair?"

"I'll check with them." Jack paused. "Can I come over?"

"Now?" She couldn't believe he'd want to see her again tonight. "You just left."

"How can we make the connection if we don't...make the connection?"

Knowing just what he had in mind, she smiled. "You always were insatiable." And she loved him for it.

"Unlock your window. I'll be right there."

"No way. Come to the front door. You're liable to get shot otherwise. Aunt Emily's taken up shooting, just in case that Hellion guy ever showed his face around here."

"Tell her I'll be right there."

"She's gone to bed. She'll recognize your car's engine

anyway. You can't stay the night though."

"That's fine. I just need to talk with you some more. See you in a few."

Immediately someone knocked on the front door. Had to be Jack. She threw on her underclothes, jeans, and a shirt, and hurried into the hall before he woke her aunt. Seeing Aunt Emily coming out of her room, Dottie quickly said, "I've got it."

Her aunt just smiled, then slipped back into her room, and shut the door.

Dottie opened the front door to see a smiling Jack. "You've been parked out front all of this time?" Unable to hide her surprise, Dottie let Jack into the house.

"Yeah. Well, not all of this time. I hoped we could talk. My family wants to see the kids."

"You said that already."

"I wanted to see you."

She grabbed his hand and led him back to the bedroom. "Do you have condoms that work better than the last time?"

He chuckled. "Fresh new pack I just picked up at the store on the way over here. I didn't want you to think I had this planned all along."

"I always loved how prepared you were for anything."

59

"Frankly, not for the fact I was to learn I have a set of twins."

"I hope it's not too much of a shock."

"No. I'm ready to be a father."

"What about us?"

"Why do you think I'm over here now?"

Dottie couldn't believe she was going to make love to Jack. Not that she hadn't thought of it, maybe later...a couple of days later. Maybe. From the time they had first met so many years ago, she'd wanted this with him. She thought at the time it was because she wanted to feel attractive to another man—after her boyfriend dumped her to join the navy—like she had been attracted to Jack. She thought it would be a quick letdown and then she'd get it out of her system. One day had led to three months of days and nights, and she realized she hadn't ever gotten him out of her system.

It felt right to be with him like this again. Seeing her Aunt Emily. The kids meeting their father and having fun with him. She wouldn't be doing this with him now if she didn't feel they could work something out between them and have a real future.

She closed her bedroom door and she realized how

white and frilly her room was when she visited her aunt—the white lace curtains and sheers, the bed covered in white eyelet, the white lace bed skirt, even the hand-painted furniture was covered in pastel flowers in pinks and lilacs. Jack didn't seem to care anything about the décor. Only about her as they began to kiss.

He removed her shirt, then kissed her cheeks, her lips, her forehead. Heat pooled in her belly as she worked to unfasten his belt. He kissed her mouth again, his hand sliding up the nape of her neck, and she gave into his rousing kiss. He lit her fire when no man had ever come close to making her feel so out of control, so needy, so willing to take this all the way.

He yanked off his jeans and fished something out of his pocket.

"Thought you'd get lucky," she whispered against his lips, pulling him in for another kiss, glad he was prepared.

His blue eyes were darkened with lust, his breathing raspy as he pulled off her jeans and tossed them aside. "Brand new," he reminded her, before he unfastened her bra and pulled it off, then ran his hands over her breasts in a loving caress. "Amazing." Then he pressed kisses all over her breasts, licking the nipples, suckling one, then the other.

When he made her feel this good, she didn't think she could last three months without his kisses. Without his loving touch.

She ran her hand over his boxer briefs, straining over his erection. She molded her hand to his hard length. He growled low and slipped his hand inside her panties and began to stroke her between her legs. She moaned at the way his touch was unravelling her self-control. "Hurry," she ground out, yanking the covers aside, then settling against the mattress.

He pulled off her panties and began stroking her faster, harder.

And then the waves of sheer pleasure rocked her world and she basked in the feeling before she yanked off his boxer briefs. Seeing his cock stretched out to her, she was going to offer to roll on the brand new condom, and stroke him a bit. Jack quickly rolled it on and moved over her like a hungry, male cat, slowly pushing his erection between her legs. Entering her. Then thrusting and she couldn't believe how good it was to feel him wrapped fully in her embrace. Excitement flared deep within her as she felt another orgasm building and begging for release.

***

God, Jack loved Dottie. He'd thought maybe he'd just fantasized about how good it was with her. He hadn't felt this way with anyone but her in years. She had been in his every waking thought and in his dreams at night. Now, here in the flesh, they had the same riveting connection as before. He couldn't let go of the need to pleasure her, to be with her, to share in the joys of life, and get through the difficult times too.

He speared her mouth with his tongue, slowing his thrusts, making them last, glad she was willing to make love with him her first night back.

He began to thrust again, unable to hold back and then he released. Warmth and satisfaction filled him, made him want to wake up to her and make love all over again.

He wanted to tell her he loved her. Still, he was afraid she wasn't ready to hear that yet. He was afraid to push her away.

He rolled off her and left the bed to dispose of the condom. He wanted to spend the night with her like they used to do. Like the father of her children would do. He wasn't sure Dottie was ready for that. He figured Aunt Emily would be though.

When he returned to the bed, Dottie pulled aside the

sheets and comforter, her silent offer to him saying he could stay a while longer. He didn't hesitate to join her in bed, pulling her into his arms, and holding her close before he wrapped them in the covers.

She kissed his chest. "I hope you don't have plans to sleep the rest of the night."

He smiled and hugged her closer. This is what he needed. "Not when I learned you were coming to see your Aunt Emily. I fully intended to give up all sleep, if I could be with you."

"I suspect my aunt will be delighted you stayed the night. We can have breakfast and then go to the theme park in the morning."

"I want to tell the kids I'm their father. Or you can tell them. Whichever way you feel is the best way to handle it."

She didn't say anything for a moment.

"Dottie?"

"I was thinking. I'll tell them over breakfast. And you can tell them whatever you'd like to say."

"Do you think we'll confuse them when I don't go home with you when you return to Yuma Town? Be disappointed?"

"You'll tell them the truth. You have to be away in the army for another three months. And then hopefully you'll come back to see them after that."

"Or you can come and see me at Fort Hood. Unless I'm out of the country, which I shouldn't be with so little time left, I'll have time to spend with you and the kids in the evenings and on the weekends. You can stay at my house in Killeen. As long as I'm not scheduled to be in the field. There's no reason for us to be apart the whole time."

"I have to work. I can't take off that much time away."

"Okay, well, let's just see. If we can, great. And if we can't, know that I'll be there as soon as I separate from the military."

She sighed and snuggled against him. "All right."

He thought she wasn't sure he was being honest with her, not after all she'd been through, but he was. He couldn't wait to find a job on the outside, and join her and the kids. He was ready to start a new career with a family. "The first time I met you, you were throwing darts at a dart board in an Irish pub with a girlfriend and you didn't even hit the target once. Though you were trying awfully hard. You looked angry, and I just sipped my beer, watching you for a while, wondering if I should get involved."

Dottie smiled at him. "Then you came over and showed me how to do it right. I still couldn't hit the target. Too many

Tom Collins. You didn't tell me right away that you were going into the army within a few months."

"You'd just broken up with a guy who was going into the navy and we really weren't sharing that much, except I had broken up with the woman I was with too. Most of all, we had agreed it was just a one-night stand. We both just needed companionship for the night."

"That lasted months. I just couldn't resist you even back then."

"Thank God for small miracles." Jack pulled her close and kissed the top of her head. "You've been in my thoughts ever since we parted ways." Unfortunately, they would be again soon.

***

Early the next morning, Jack and Dottie got up before the kids did so they didn't see Jack coming out of her bedroom. "Did you tell your family you weren't coming home last night?" Dottie asked, as she started to make pancakes.

"I didn't tell them exactly. When I said I was going back to your place to speak with you further, I'm sure they assumed I wasn't returning, especially when I didn't return. My sister texted me this morning. Dad has to work. Mom and my sister want to see you and the kids and your aunt and so they'll meet us at the park."

"Okay, sounds great."

Aunt Emily came into the kitchen, all smiles. "Morning, you two."

"Morning," Jack said, getting her a cup of coffee.

"Okay, I'm going to tell the kids you're their dad. I don't know how this will go over with them, because they might think you're going to start living with us. Like dads live with moms and their kids."

Jack smiled. "I'm game."

Dottie shook her head. "What if you don't want to leave the service in three months? Or you only want to be with us just because you feel a family obligation to be with the kids."

"I've always wanted to see you...way before I learned you had the kids."

Emily was setting the table, quiet, trying not to be intrusive.

"All right, but it might not work out between us and then the kids will wonder why you don't live with us."

"So you don't want to tell them I'm their father until I return from the service?"

Dottie flipped a couple of pancakes onto a platter. "No, they need to know. I'm just saying it might be hard for them to understand."

"I understand. I'll let you handle it as you see fit." He hoped she would tell them and they wouldn't be upset to learn he was their daddy, then be unable to see them for what, to them, might seem like forever. "I'd be more than willing to have you visit me at Fort Hood. I'll pay for airfare too."

"You won't have any leave time so you can't take off to see us." Dottie scooped some more pancakes onto the platter.

"True. I want to save the rest of my leave so I can take them as terminal leave and be out in three months."

"Which means they could have you out in the field for some of the time that you have left."

"You're right."

"Without much notice."

"Uh, yeah." Sometimes they called them for a drill in the middle of the night to see just how prepared the units were for mobilization.

"So it could work out, but it might not at all. I'd hate to waste your money flying us out there to spend time with you and then we can't be together. It wouldn't be much fun for any of us."

"Okay, that's true." He could never predict what his work schedule would be like.

They heard the kids hurrying down the hall, their slippers slapping at the wood floor as they ran for the kitchen. They were still wearing their PJ shorts and shirts and hurried to give Dottie a hug.

"Pancakes!" the kids both said, eyeing them with interest.

"Before we eat breakfast, I have something to tell you." Dottie's voice was serious sounding, and the kids both riveted their attention from the stack of pancakes on the platter to their mom.

"Aww, we're not going to go to the park?" Jeff complained.

"We're going after we eat breakfast. I need to tell you something about Jack. I haven't really ever said who your real father is." She motioned to Jack. "Jack is your real father."

Jeff and Trish looked at Jack as if they couldn't believe it. They acted almost as if they hadn't seen him before.

"You can call him daddy or dad," she said.

"Okay," Jeff said. "Can we eat now? Aunt Emily said we can ride on the airplane ride."

Jack chuckled. He had no idea what to expect, yet on the

other hand, he should have guessed. He suspected that's how he would have reacted if he'd been their age. Even if they'd fed them first, they were too excited to go to the park so he imagined telling them after they ate wouldn't have made any difference either.

"We're going to see your grandmother and your Aunt Roberta," Dottie said. "Your granddad won't be there because he has to work. We'll see him later."

"Cool," Jeff said.

Trish nodded.

An hour and half later when they finally arrived at the theme park, they met up with Jack's sister and his mother and they made introductions. Tears in her eyes, his mom was the first to hug the kids and then Roberta did.

"Jeff looks just like you when you were that age, Jack," his mother said.

"They never met my parents," Dottie said. "So I'm glad they get to meet all of you."

"We couldn't be happier," Lisa said. "And John can't wait to see you and the kids later too. He was disappointed he couldn't take off from work to see them today."

"We'll be sure to get together," Emily said. "We'd love for you to come to the zoo and the Renaissance fair with us too."

It wasn't long after they had taken the kids on a couple of kiddie rides at Roberta's urging, that she suddenly motioned to a blond-haired guy standing near an ice cream stand. "Oh, there's Phillip."

Jack wondered what the chances were that an old boyfriend would show up at the theme park with his own sister and her kids and Roberta would see him right off. "I thought you ditched him a couple of years ago."

"I did. It doesn't mean I can't say hi."

Jack smiled at her and just shook his head.

"Trish wants to go on the merry-go-round," Dottie said. "Jeff wants to go on the kiddie airplane ride. It's just around the corner."

"I'll take Jeff," Jack said, "and I'll meet you over here afterward."

"I'll stay with you, Dottie," Aunt Emily said.

Jack's mother was looking at a shop window filled with hand carvings.

Roberta had already headed off to see her old boyfriend. He was with his sister, her two kids, and their mother. Jack figured they were having a family get-together too. He couldn't remember why she had dumped Phillip. As far as Jack recalled, he was a nice enough guy.

Jack was happy to take Jeff on the kiddy rides. He'd never imagined doing this with his own kids anytime soon.

"How'd you like the plane trip here?" Jack asked, as he and Jeff moved into line for the ride.

"It was fun. Mommy gave us coloring books and we colored, though we were up so early, we fell asleep first." Jeff watched the airplanes slow to a standstill.

"I want to do all kinds of things with you and Trish and your mom, and Aunt Emily, before you return to Colorado."

"Cool."

"I'll have to go back to Fort Hood to do more work. When I'm through, I want to see you and Trish and your mom so I can take you fishing and swimming, boating, camping, everything you'd love to do."

"Riding the ponies?"

"Can you teach me how? I've never been on a horse before."

"Yeah."

Jack smiled. "I'd love that. While I'm gone, I'll call you and Trish and your mom."

"Okay."

Jack hadn't known what to expect from the kids.

Sometimes they talked his ear off. Right now, Jeff was too excited about getting on the ride. Jack looked forward to the day when the kids were older, and he could actually ride with Jeff and Trish on some of the grownup rides. They'd take the train later though.

When the other kids left their miniature airplanes, Jack said, "I'm going to take pictures of you. So wave when you go by."

Jeff nodded, then he and the other kids in line ran to their planes. Once Jeff was seated in a bright yellow one and was belted in, the ride took off and at a small child's pace, it went up and down and around. Jeff waved at Jack when the plane went around each time, and Jack snapped as many shots as he could get. After a few minutes, the ride came to a stop and the kids got off.

Jeff ran straight to Jack, grabbed his hand, and tugged at him to go back in line. "Can we do it again?" Jeff asked so eagerly, Jack said he could.

Jeff hurried to get back in line, pulling Jack along with him. As soon as they were waiting to get on again, Jack texted Dottie: Jeff's going on the airplane ride again and then we'll join you.

Dottie texted back: Okay, we'll go on the carousel again.

Jack was glad they could do it like this, separate and let the kids go to the different rides instead of having to go to one that the other didn't care for. Though they would have to learn to take turns getting on rides they might not be as eager to try.

As soon as Jeff returned from the ride the second time, they headed back to the carousel. Jack met up with Dottie. There was no sign of his mom or Aunt Emily. Roberta was still talking to her old boyfriend while the rest of Phillip's family had taken off.

"Where's my mom?" Jack asked, thinking she might have gone into the store filled with wood carvings.

"I thought she'd gone with you." Dottie glanced back at the store.

"I'll check inside." He called his mom on her cell phone while he headed for the store. She didn't pick up. Maybe she didn't hear the phone because of all the noise at the theme park between people screaming on the rides, the rackety-rack noise of the rides, and the country and western music playing at the different buildings that were serving food or offering entertainment. The cougars' hearing was better. That also meant they heard more noise.

He walked into the store and moved around high racks

of wood carvings. His mom wasn't there. Maybe she went to the restroom. He texted her. No response to that either.

He returned to Dottie and the kids and her aunt. "Not in there and I can't reach her on her phone. Maybe she went into the restroom near here?"

"I'll go check." Aunt Emily headed for the closest one while they waited.

"You're not worried about her, are you?" Dottie sounded a little concerned herself.

"No. If she can't find us, she'll go to the Lost and Found."

Dottie smiled. "Do you have experience with this?"

"Only once. But we lost Roberta that time when she was thirteen. Someone on the staff had taken her to the Lost and Found. Mom knows where that is."

Before Aunt Emily reached them, she was shaking her head. "She's not in the ladies' room."

"Everybody has a phone, right?" Jack asked. "I'll grab my sister and we can search for her if you want to go to a ride and just keep us informed of where you'll be."

"We'll help you search for her," Dottie said. "I'll take the kids to the Lost and Found while you check with your sister."

"I'll stay with Dottie. I don't want us all to get separated," Emily said.

"Okay. We'll search around the area close to where we were when we were all together." Jack headed off to see Roberta and said hello to Phillip, explaining their Mom was lost.

Roberta rolled her eyes.

Jack frowned at her. "Hey, you were lost here once before."

Roberta's jaw dropped, and Jack suspected she hadn't wanted him to tell on her like that. He didn't think it was any big deal. Scary for everyone. Nothing to be ashamed of.

"Isn't she answering her phone?" Roberta asked. "Oh, don't tell me. She forgot it at home again."

"Great. Well, I looked in the shop with the wood-carved figures, the last place I saw her. She wasn't inside, and Aunt Emily looked in the restroom. Dottie and the kids and her aunt are going to the Lost and Found to see if Mom's there."

"I'll help you look for her." Phillip sounded like he wanted to spend some more time with Roberta. Unless he planned to look for Mom on his own, and he was trying to come up with an excuse to get away from Roberta. To Jack's surprise, Phillip wrapped his arm around her shoulders as if to say they were doing this together. Then again, he thought about how Dottie and he had gone their separate ways and were trying to make something of their relationship again.

"Thanks. I'm going to head this way." Jack motioned to the path that led west.

"We'll go away from the path that would lead to the Lost and Found," his sister said, and then they took off.

About twenty minutes later, Dottie texted him: She's not at the Lost and Found and she hasn't been here.

Jack called Dottie. "Roberta and her old boyfriend Phillip are headed south. I'm going west. Wait, I see her. I think." And it was bad news. His ex-fiancée was talking to his mother, Gigi's hands on her hips, her blond hair swept back in a ponytail, while his mom had her arms folded across her waist, frowning, her mouth pursed.

He stalked forward to rescue his mother from Gigi's apparent tirade.

"Your rotten son put my brother in jail!"

"Your rotten brother put himself in jail, right where he belongs. What do you think would have happened to your brother if he had shot and killed my son that day? Huh? He's just lucky Jack had enough hand-to-hand combat training that he disarmed your brother and kept him from hurting him and he didn't hurt Hellion either. As for you, you're nothing but--"

Jack quickly interceded before his mother said anything more. Gigi just stared at him as if she couldn't believe he'd be here. Which, if he'd been working, he wouldn't have been. She raised her hand to slap his face. He quickly grabbed her arm. "I'll call the police and swear out a complaint against you if I have to," he growled at Gigi.

"You would too." Gigi's green eyes were darkened in anger, her mouth curved down.

"You're damn right." Jack released her wrist and turned to his mom and gave her a hug. "Are you all right?"

"Yes. I'm fine. Where are your mate and your adorable kids?"

He couldn't believe his mother would antagonize Gigi by making up a story about Dottie, or mention his having kids. His mother was normally so mild-mannered, except she'd always felt Gigi and her family were bad news. She'd been right.

Jack led her away from Gigi. "Mom, we thought we'd lost you," he said, as if she hadn't known that. Maybe she hadn't realized it yet, if she thought they were still where'd they'd been a few minutes ago.

"I saw you near the carousal, and it looked like the kids were going to ride it, so I went to the glass blower's booth and went inside to look at the glassware in the shop. Right as I was coming out of the shop, Gigi stopped me to harass me. I didn't even recognize her at first. If she hadn't corralled me and I couldn't have found you, I would have gone to the Lost and Found."

"Are you sure you're fine? Gigi didn't touch you, did she?"

"No, Jack. I'm really okay. She just went ballistic when she saw me. It was just a shock to see her and to hear her tirade. If she'd gotten physical with me, I would have screamed for the police."

He texted everyone to let them know he had found his mom. And that Gigi was here harassing her. Dottie and the rest agreed to have lunch at the Old Cantina. Roberta said she was having lunch with Phillip at the Cabaret and would see them later tonight. Phillip would take her home. "Hey, have fun, both of you." Jack wondered how long that would last between them this time.

"Aunt Emily, Dottie, and the kids went to the Lost and Found to look for you. I tried calling you," Jack said to his mom.

"I left my phone at home. You know me, I forget to charge it up, so I had it charging, and then I forgot to bring it."

"Okay, no problem. We can all get together and eat lunch then. Roberta is visiting with Phillip."

His mom's brows rose. "Her old boyfriend?"

"Yeah, surprised me too. They were both looking for you also."

"I'm so sorry that I lost you," Lisa said.

"No problem." Still, Jack took a relieved breath, and then saw the rest of the gang headed their way.

He glanced back at where Gigi had been, figuring she might have been watching them to see who his wife and kids were, but she had slowly followed them. He'd hoped she'd taken off. He just hoped she didn't get into a fight with them. He would call security if she harassed any of them further.

Dottie took hold of Jack's hand and kissed his cheek, whispering seductively in his ear, "You can pretend we barely know each other, or we can give her a real eyeful."

"I agree," Aunt Emily said.

"Mom already told her we were a couple and the kids are mine."

"I sure like your mom," Emily said.

Jack smiled at her.

"Mommy said we had to hold hands all the time," Jeff

said to Lisa as if she needed someone to watch over her better.

His mom took hold of Jeff's hand, and Emily took hold of his other. "Then you can make sure I don't get lost."

"Did you get scared?" Trish asked, hugging Lisa.

His mom's eyes filled with tears as she hugged Trish back with her free hand. "If a woman hadn't been talking my ear off, I might have been. But Jack found me right away."

Jeff and Trish looked at her ears.

Jack hadn't realized the kids took comments so literally. "We won't lose the two of you. We know everything you're up to. We have eyes in the back of our heads to keep a watch on the two of you."

"No, you don't," Trish said.

Jeff had to take a look to see. "No, you don't," Jeff agreed.

Everyone laughed.

Jack lifted Trish onto his hip, wrapped his arm around Dottie's shoulders, and leaned down to give her a real kiss. They definitely looked like they were one happy family. And he liked feeling this way.

After that, they headed to the restaurant to eat.

"Okay, so why in the world is she harassing your mom?"

Dottie asked. "It's been more than five years since you broke off the engagement with her, for heaven's sake."

"Yeah, I never gave her another thought. I never believed she'd be here or hassle my mom or any of us. Maybe scowl at me if she saw me when I was running around town. That's about it. If I'd even given her a thought, I would have believed she'd gotten married already herself."

"She has been," Lisa said. "Twice before. I saw the wedding announcements in the paper. Maybe two years apart?"

"Can you imagine what it would have been like if you'd married her?" Aunt Emily asked.

"Horrible," Dottie said, answering for Jack.

He just smiled at them as they made their way into the restaurant. He did wonder why Gigi was here at the theme park by herself. Though he'd come here with her a few times when they were dating. Was she dating someone then? If so, why was she harassing his mom? His mom didn't have anything to do with Gigi's brother going to jail.

When the hostess escorted them to their seats at the Old Cabana, he saw Gigi come into the restaurant with a guy, shaggy brown hair, jeans, black T-shirt featuring a white skull.

"Is she stalking us?" Lisa asked.

"Looks like it. Otherwise, why come to this restaurant? Why not go somewhere else?" Dottie asked.

"Looks like she has a new boyfriend." Lisa put her napkin on her lap. "You'd think that would satisfy her."

Dottie began reading the menu to the kids so they could decide what they wanted.

Jack studied Dottie and his son and daughter for a moment, realizing how this was the first time he'd taken his kids out to a restaurant, and how much he loved that they were going to be able to share lots of first times together, once he moved close to Dottie in Yuma Town.

"Don't look now. That guy who's with that woman is headed toward our table." Aunt Emily grabbed up her phone, and he knew she was getting ready to call the police, or at least threaten to call them.

Jack turned to see if the guy truly was coming to confront him or not. Sure enough, he was headed straight for Jack while Gigi was standing in the waiting area, her arms folded across her chest, as if she was still waiting with the other customers for a table.

Jack rose from his chair, nodded in greeting. He remained serious in case this became ugly. He was going to ask him to step outside to talk if the guy became belligerent.

The guy held out his hand, surprising Jack. He shook it in good faith.

"Okay, listen, my name is Al, and Gigi said you were harassing her when I went to the men's room."

"She's a liar," Lisa jumped in to say. "She was threatening me because her brother tried to kill my son, and then Jack testified to help put the guy away. He used a gun in a burglary first, then threatened my son with it."

"Well, I didn't believe her. Not when you're here with a family and you came into the restaurant before we did. I mean, how can you be stalking her if we followed you in here? I just wanted to get the facts straight," Al said. "She said that you were seeing someone else when you were engaged to her, Jack. And by the looks of it, you got the other woman pregnant."

"She'll tell you whatever she wants you to hear," Jack said. "She's the one who had three boyfriends on the side when we were engaged. When I learned of it, I broke it off with her. A few weeks later, I met Dottie. That was five years ago. Gigi needs to get over it."

"She's been married twice herself already. If she'd wanted to be with my son, and only my son, they would have been married. Just be careful around that one. Her brother is a real psycho," Lisa warned.

"I've heard about her brother, trumped up charges. He was the fall guy. He didn't do anything." Al frowned. "Gigi was married twice? She told me she'd only been married once."

"You can do a search on the Internet. It's all right there in black and white." Lisa drank some of her water. "Same with his criminal charges. Not trumped up at all."

"Thanks, I wanted to just learn what was going on. I'll let you get on with your lunch." Al offered his hand to Jack and they shook.

"Sorry, man, that you had to get involved in her stuff like this."

"Hey, I'm used to it." Al smiled at Dottie. "I just need to find the right woman for me."

Then he turned and headed back to where Gigi was waiting. She frowned at him and began to say something. He brushed past her and left the restaurant. After giving Jack a growly look, she turned and hurried after her newest boyfriend. Or maybe, her already ex-boyfriend.

Jack wondered how long that was going to last, if it wasn't over already. He hoped the guy would make a quick escape from the relationship, much sooner than Jack had. He retook his seat and the waitress returned to take their orders.

After they ordered and the waitress left, Jack said, "I wonder if Gigi harasses the men she married and their families also."

"Who knows? Maybe it was her idea to divorce them. I suspect if it's her idea, she doesn't have any problem with it. If it's the guy's idea, she can't deal with it," his mother said.

"At least they left the restaurant." Jack placed his napkin on his lap, glad that he was going to be living in Yuma Town near Dottie and not anywhere near his crazy ex-fiancée.

Forty minutes later when Jack was paying for the meal, he received a call from security at the theme park. Now what?

"I'm Tim Edwards, head of security at the park. Is this Jack Barrington?"

"Yeah. What's the problem?" Jack suspected it all had to do with Gigi.

"A woman named Gigi Crichton said you threatened her boyfriend, and he was so afraid to be with her, he left the park without her."

Jack couldn't believe it. Along with her brother, the woman was certifiable. "I don't know Al's last name. We had a nice, congenial chat, and he left. He seems to me like he has a good head on his shoulders. She was trying to get him riled up to confront me for something that didn't happen. If you want to know his side of the story, you'll have to speak with him. But we shook hands and there was no trouble at all. As to another matter, she was verbally abusive to my mother before I rescued her from Gigi's tirade."

"Okay, thanks, Mr. Barrington."

They finished the call and Jack paid the bill.

"What was *that* all about?" Dottie asked.

"Gigi's new boyfriend left her at the park without a ride. Serves her right for sending him to threaten me."

Everyone agreed.

After a long day of rides, the last one on the train, they headed home, the kids were tired, but they'd had a great time. Except for Gigi and her nonsense, they'd all enjoyed the day. He thought he really suited being a dad.

They had dinner with his family after that so that his dad could meet the kids. He was just as thrilled to be their granddaddy as Jack was to be their daddy. He believed they could really be a permanent family when he was through with the army.

***

The next two and a half weeks meant runs with the kids as cougars, a paddle wheeler trip, a visit to the zoo, and finally the Renaissance fair. Up until today, both his parents, his sister, and Dottie's aunt had been coming to some of the activities.

Today was Dottie and the kids' last day here. Tomorrow, they were taking them to the airport. And he had to leave the day after so he could save up his leave time for Dottie and the kids.

"I can't believe the whole family bowed out of going to the fair with us today," Dottie said, helping Trish into her purple and green fairy princess gown.

Jack was helping Jeff dress in his Robin Hood costume—velvet-like green vest, blue jeans, cowboy boots, and a green velvet Robin Hood hat complete with feather.

Aunt Emily had even bought a medieval gown for Dottie—a lovely dark blue gown with lots of gold braid that made her look like a princess. She purchased it through an online store, but they only had clothes for women and Jack wasn't sure he wanted to dress up. Certainly not if he had to wear tights.

"You look like a princess," he said, pulling Dottie close and kissing her.

"What about your costume?" Jeff asked.

"I'll probably pick up something at the fair." Not that Jack really intended to. He figured the kids would be so caught up in all the sights and fun that they wouldn't really think about what he was wearing.

"We'll help your daddy pick out something that he'd like." Dottie gave him a little smile that said he wasn't getting out of dressing up like the rest of them.

He laughed.

Then they left the house and drove to the fairgrounds. But Dottie wasn't letting Jack off the hook about the costume business and took him into a leather store first. Leather arm bands and leggings were a start. Leather boots. This wasn't so bad. As long as he didn't have to wear Robin Hood tights. A white peasant shirt and a hat with a feather in it completed the ensemble. He really did feel the part when Renaissance fairgoers welcomed the family.

And that's what they truly were. He realized that was probably some of the reason his family and Aunt Emily bowed out of going with them today. They'd wanted them to do something as a real family. Just the four of them. Begin to have some real shared experiences and make some new memories.

They watched the comedic shows, listened to singers and watched dancers, and saw the knights jousting. Jeff wanted to be a knight when he grew up. "Uncle Hal could even give me a horse like that one." He pointed to the palomino.

Jack agreed that would make a great knight's horse.

"Why don't you fight the bad knight?" Jeff asked, looking up at Jack as if he truly believed all of this was real.

"Well, I wouldn't get very far, I'm afraid. I've never ridden a horse, remember?"

Jeff's eyes grew big. "I forgot. Uncle Hal will teach you how to ride a pony when you come to live with us. You can ride one of his ponies until you know how to do it and then you can ride a big horse."

Riding horses wasn't something Jack had ever thought he'd do. But for his son, he'd definitely give it a try.

After they watched the joust, they had pizza and ice cream cones, watched a couple of more shows, then headed home. When they arrived at Aunt Emily's, she had dinner waiting for them and treated them as if they were special medieval guests. She smiled at Jack. "I love all that leather."

"So do I," Dottie said, hurrying into the kitchen to help serve up the food.

Chicken drumlets, mashed potatoes and gravy, green beans, and chocolate cake were eaten with relish. The kids told all about the exciting day they'd had and after baths and putting them to bed, Jack asked if Dottie wanted to go for a run. He rarely was able to run as a cougar unless he did so when he came home on leave. It just wasn't safe for him to do it when he was stationed at Fort Hood, or most places where he'd been assigned.

"I'm going to miss doing this with you and having my aunt to help out. Maybe we can run with the kids in the morning before we fly out in the afternoon. They love to run with you, but they were too tired tonight."

"I'd like that."

She smiled. "They've been having so much fun, they don't want it to end."

"And you?""

"Especially me."

He was so glad to hear it. Now if nothing came between them while he was away, he thought they had a real chance together as a family. The time had gone by so quickly that Jack couldn't believe it was nearly time for Dottie and the kids to return home.

Dottie and Jack drove out to their favorite spot in the

woods and hid their clothes as usual, shifted, and ran. He chased her tail and tried to capture it as she waved it back and forth like a flag in a teasing way. But man was she fast. Still, he could take her down with one powerful, male cougar leap, and he did.

She came up play fighting, but he pinned her down and licked her muzzle. She licked him back. He'd miss her and the kids terribly until they were together again. He'd always had high hopes he'd get together with her. Now with having seen her and gotten to know her all over again, as well as the kids, he knew he'd want even more time with them.

They laid together for a long while, just enjoying being cougars until she finally sighed and licked his cheek and rose to her feet.

They returned home and made love half the night. He loved waking up with her snuggled against him. He was certain she was feeling the same as him, and he couldn't wait to get out of the army.

The next day, he and her aunt took them to the airport. It was heart-wrenching for the kids, who felt they were losing their daddy when they'd never really had one. Both Jeff and Trish cried, and that made Emily and Dottie all teary-eyed also. Jack too.

He promised he'd talk to them on the phone and on Skype, send presents even, if he couldn't see them before he left the service.

Dottie hugged him and kissed him like she couldn't get enough of him. If he didn't have to return to Fort Hood, he would have been flying out with them today to Yuma Town.

"I've had such a lovely time with all of you," her aunt said, kissing and hugging the kids, then Dottie.

"Same here," Dottie said. "We won't wait so long to see you the next time."

"Good."

When Dottie and the kids took off for security checks at the airport, Jack was feeling a multitude of emotions between wishing she and the kids didn't have to leave, and he didn't have to go, to being eager to get his remaining obligation over with.

"You'd better keep in touch with Dottie and the kids like you said you would," Aunt Emily warned, as if she had to tell him. "You can't disappoint them. They truly love you."

"I won't." Jack smiled at her and took her arm as he led her back to the parking lot. "As long as I'm not in the field or working where I can't contact them, I'll be in touch."

"Are you glad I convinced Dottie to come here with the

kids?"

Jack chuckled. "I think you know the answer to that question and as soon as I join her and the kids in Yuma Town, I'm asking her to marry me. So, hell yeah, I was glad to see her and Trish and Jeff and happy to be given the chance to prove how much I care about all of them and want to be with them as soon as I can."

Three months would feel like a lifetime.

CHAPTER 4

As soon as Dottie and the kids arrived at the airport, she called Jack to tell him they made it home.

"I'll be leaving first thing in the morning, and I'll give you and the kids a call when I get in."

"Okay, sounds good. Stryker Hill, our full-time deputy sheriff, is here to pick us up at the airport. I'll call you later when we're home again."

"Okay, I'm just chilling with Aunt Emily. I look forward to getting your call."

Dottie and Jack ended the call, and she hurried with the kids to see Stryker, who was all smiles, his green eyes cheerful, his wavy dark hair freshly cut. She felt her smile was strained. She and the kids had a wonderful vacation. Now she needed to tell her friends the truth about Jack Barrington.

"We're having a big welcome home for you at Hal and Tracey's ranch," Stryker said, hauling out their bags to his vehicle.

She and the kids were tired. But she knew she couldn't say no to her friends.

"I'm taking you straight to the ranch. I warned everyone you and the kids would probably be tired. All your friends wanted to show you how glad they were that you were coming home and how much they missed you."

"I missed everyone too." Though she'd been so busy with Jack and her aunt and his family, she'd been rather occupied. If Jack hadn't been in her bed every night, she would have thought of them then too. She'd missed him the moment she and the kids left him to go to the security checkpoint at the airport. Tonight when she went to bed all alone, she'd miss him all over again. Even at the ranch, she wanted what the other couples had. A mate to snuggle with at the fire pit and to take home with her that night when the celebration was over. A daddy who would help her put the kids to bed. And then kiss her senseless all over again.

"Can we ride the ponies?" Jeff asked, perking up.

"I'm sure Hal's foreman would be happy to take you and Trish for a ride," Stryker said, smiling down at Jeff. "You know how much Ted Weekum loves to take kids on rides."

"Daddy doesn't know how to ride. He's not a kid, but I told him Uncle Hal would teach him how to ride on a pony first."

Stryker looked at Dottie, waiting to hear what this was all about. She'd told the kids not to say anything to anyone about their daddy until she'd had a chance to tell everyone. But she halfway figured one or both of them would let it slip.

"Tell you when we get there," Dottie told Stryker. She didn't want to have to repeat what she was going to say to everyone over and over again.

"All right. So what did you get to do while you were at your Aunt Emily's?" Stryker asked.

Jeff started digging in his suitcase. "I got to be Robin Hood and mommy was a princess." He waved his Robin Hood hat about.

"I was a fairy princess," Trish said, snuggling with her cloth doll in the back seat. "And Daddy was..."

"He was a knight. But he doesn't know how to ride a horse," Jeff said.

Stryker again took his eyes off the road and glanced at Dottie.

"I'll tell everyone when we sit down to talk," she said.

Stryker shook his head, but he was smirking.

When they arrived at the horse ranch, everyone welcomed her back with a big barbecue—Hal and Tracey Haverton, owners of the ranch. Chase and Shannon Buchanan, who ran the Pinyon Pines Resort, the newly renovated cabins at Lake Buchanan that had been in his family for generations, and their two-year-old twins, Zoey and Sadie, who both gave Jeff and Trish a hug, excited to see them back. Dan Steinacker, her boss and the sheriff; Stryker Hill, the deputy sheriff; Travis and Bridget MacKay, Cougar Special Forces Division agents; and Leyton Hill, also a CSF agent, and his mate, Dr. Kate Parker, the only physician in town. Leyton and Stryker had recently learned they were twin brothers and that had shaken them up a bit. Not to mention Ted Weekum, the foreman, and the ranch hands, Ricky and his older brother, Kolby Jones were there to celebrate Dottie and the kids' return.

The whole time on the flight home, she'd been rehearsing how she was going to tell them about Jack Barrington. Stryker hadn't said a word to anyone about the daddy business, waiting for her to get settled and tell the story.

Now she was seated with the rest of the adults around

the fire pit, beers or glasses of wine in hand. All except Tracey, who was pregnant with twins, and Kate, who were both drinking sweet tea.

"Did you have fun with your Aunt Emily?" Dr. Kate asked Dottie, snuggling with Leyton on one of the outdoor couches, a fire blazing in the fire pit.

Ted offered to take Jeff and Trish to ride ponies in a little corral nearby. The kids, wanting to show off their Renaissance costumes, had dressed at the ranch house first. Ted had made a big deal of addressing Trish as a princess and Jeff as Master Robin.

"I'm Robin Hood," Jeff said, as if Ted had gotten his name wrong.

"Why yes, of course. Master Robin Hood."

"Can you teach Daddy how to ride a pony?"

"Yeah, cuz he doesn't know how to ride one," Trish said.

Everyone turned their attention from the kids to Dottie, some with raised eyebrows. Dan was frowning, his blue eyes narrowed, his dark brown hair shaggier than she'd ever seen it. He was unshaven too, and dark circles beneath his eyes revealed he hadn't been getting enough sleep.

"Uh, yeah, we had a really good time," Dottie told everyone gathered. "I have some news though. I ran into someone I knew back in college, Jack Barrington. I have to tell you something that I've kept from everyone. I'm glad to be able to tell you now. Jeffrey Brown was not the father of my kids. He made me promise to say they were and I didn't know if I'd ever see Jack again. He's been in the army all of this time and was Trish and Jeff's biological father. I *mean,* Jack *is* their father."

Everyone sat in silence, just watching her, waiting to see what else she had to say about this revelation. "I didn't tell anyone because Jack wanted to make an army career of it at the time. I didn't want to be hauled from one assignment to another. It's difficult enough for a military wife, who isn't used to the military, but it really is problematic when you're a cougar. And even more so when you have cougar children. I don't know how he's managed to deal with not being able to run as a cougar for months at a time."

"We did fine," Leyton said, just one of the few men here who had served in the military. It was a time-honored tradition for the men of Yuma Town. But they didn't mate anyone until they left the service.

She appreciated the military and the men and women for their service. She just had not wanted to be married to an active duty service member. Yet after renewing her relationship with Jack, she was eager to make this work between them.

"But I understand how you would feel about moving a couple of kids around like that. For footloose bachelors, we made do," Leyton said.

Everyone knew the circumstances surrounding her cousin's death and her father's too.

All the guys agreed. Dan, Chase, Leyton, his brother, Stryker, Travis, Hal, and even Ted had served. She was afraid her boss would be upset with her for not being honest about this beforehand. Something was going on with Dan too and so she knew she hadn't been the only one keeping a big secret.

Dan took a swig of his beer. "I've known. I wasn't sure if the two of you would ever get together again. I learned of it a while back."

Shocked to the core, Dottie didn't know if he was just saying so because he was upset with her for not telling everyone the truth or he really had known. Why hadn't he told her then? "When?"

"Some time ago," he said vaguely. "I'm the sheriff. I know when something isn't adding up."

No one else said anything, just waiting for Dan to get it

off his chest. She wondered if he wasn't the only one who had known or had suspected then.

"The babies' ages? That Jeffrey Brown just showed up from nowhere, and claimed the babies were his? I didn't trust him back then. He had an air about him—that he'd served. He'd let some terminology slip that either meant he'd been in one of the branches or he had a military family. I'd asked him once. He said no. Just the way he held my gaze as if to prove to me he was telling the truth made me wary. Then he took off after the kids were born. When I looked into his background to learn what I could, to see if I could at least get him on child support, I found a dead-end. Still, I really didn't think the kids were his. After we learned about the criminal activities he was involved in, I suspected he'd used you and the kids as a cover. Still, I wanted to know who the father was, if Brown wasn't Jeff and Trish's dad. I discovered you'd been seeing a Jack Barrington in college, and that the two of you had been good friends. Then he went into the army. I know how much you weren't interested in being a military wife. But I also figured if he got out, you and he might end up together. It's for the best really, if he loves you and the kids. That's all we can ever hope for."

Everyone was quiet for a little while.

"So what do you think?" Bridget asked, sounding like she wanted to be excited for her, if this was going to work out. She was CSF and had rescued Travis at Christmastime. They'd had a quick romance, fallen in love, and mated.

"I want to be with him. He *is* good with the kids, and with me."

Shannon joined her and gave her a big hug. "I'm so excited for you. It'll work out. I know it will."

Chase gave her a hug too and agreed, then they retook their seats.

"So what's the deal then exactly? How long does he have left on active duty?" Hal was a part-time deputy, but he was doing a lot of Tracey's kind of work too and they owned the horse ranch. Both currently worked as Special Agents for the U.S. Department of Fish and Wildlife Services, going after wildlife exploiters. Though with Tracey being pregnant, she was getting lower-key assignments. She had about three and half months left before the twins arrived.

Dottie didn't know how Hal could be pulled in so many directions and still have time for Tracey. "Jack is coming here after his service obligation is up. I'd hoped maybe he could work for the sheriff's office or maybe for Leyton with the CSF. He has the combat training like all of you had."

"He would have to work for my boss, Chuck Warner, for several months to a year in White Bear Lake, Minnesota, if he got on with CSF. Jack will need the training and mentorship," Leyton said.

Travis McKay and his wife, Bridget, who both had worked for Chuck, agreed. "It's for the best," Travis said. "Nothing worse than getting yourself killed on your first mission out. And Chuck ensures he keeps his agents alive."

Dottie noted that Dan didn't offer to make Jack a deputy sheriff instead.

If Jack had to work several months to a year training with the CSF away from home? She'd never last.

***

Three months later, Jack was due to come into town and stay with Dottie, and she really thought this could work. They'd kept up correspondence, and she'd told everyone about Jack and hoped he might be able to get a job with Leyton as an agent with the CSF, sooner, than later. She thought Jack would be a quick study, though Leyton had told her time and again that it was for the best if he trained with one of the best. She thought he was one of the best.

Jack had sent comic books, coloring books, or books to read to the kids almost on a daily basis. She loved him for it, but she had to keep telling Jeff and Trish that this was only while Jack was separated from them. She didn't want them to think he was going to give them presents every day of the year when he lived with them.

No one was making a big deal of putting out the welcome mat for Jack in Yuma Town, just her. She hoped her friends would treat Jack like a friend and not the enemy here. If anyone was to blame for her not telling them that he was the father of her twins, it was her, not him. She knew it didn't have all to do with that though. They worried about her and the kids in case things didn't work out like the last time she was married. Maybe Jack needed the adventure in his life. The ability to travel all over. Maybe he wouldn't like living in one little place the rest of his life. Or the day-to-day drudgery of having a wife and kids. She loved her kids, her life, but she'd grown into the role of being a mother. It wasn't all about theme parks, zoos, and Renaissance fairs. It was all the daily stuff that a parent had to deal with.

But she was excited about seeing him as a prospective mate too. Her lover, and husband. She'd missed that time with him. Every time she'd thought about seeing him though, he'd been called out into the field and he finally had told her it would be best if he just joined her when he was free to do so.

Except now she had a new problem. She'd gone in to see Dr. Kate Parker-Hill, sure that the test results the doctor would run would say the same as the ones she'd used.

Now, Dottie sat on an exam table at the clinic. "I can handle it," she said to Kate. She'd used one of those over-the-counter pregnancy tests, well, ten of them. Though she'd bought them in Loveland so no one in Yuma Town would suspect she might be pregnant or was worried she was, when she wasn't. She had to be certain the multiple tests had told the truth though.

Damn if Kate didn't smile at her, her brows raised a bit and said, "Well, Dottie, you're pregnant. No telling if you'll have a single birth, twins, or more at this point, but yeah, you are right. It's time to put you on prenatal vitamins."

"Jack isn't going to be happy about this."

Kate raised a brow. "They're his, aren't they?"

"Yeah, of course they are. But every time he leaves, I turn up pregnant! He hasn't really had time to get used to being the father to the twins."

"Not all your fault. If you want me to, when he gets here, we can take care of that little problem."

Dottie smiled. "Oh, I'm sure he'll be thrilled. He just

comes in to Yuma Town to see me and you have him scheduled for a vasectomy. After the baby is born, and I'm sure I don't want any more, I'll haul him off to your clinic to take care of matters."

Kate smiled back. "I can do it. Clear my schedule and everything. As to the pregnancy, you said he was good with the kids."

"Yeah, but this is different."

"Right, he'll be here to help raise this baby from day one."

"That's if he can get a job. Leyton still won't let him work here. He wants him to work in White Bear Lake first."

"Join him. Then once he's had his training, return here with him, and you can all be one big happy family."

"There's no cougar town in Minnesota. Nothing near White Bear Lake."

Kate sighed. "You will both find a way to make this work. I have no doubt about it."

Dottie's phone rang, and she said, "Excuse me. It's Jack. Hopefully he didn't get delayed."

"Well, congratulations." Kate patted her shoulder. "Can't wait to meet him."

"Thanks!" Dottie left the exam room and answered the

call. "Are you nearly here?"

"I'm at a service station just outside of town. I'll be there in just a few minutes. I have some news. I'll tell you when I get there."

He sounded not real sure she'd like the news. She didn't know how he'd take her news either. She absolutely wasn't going to rely on any condoms he used ever again.

As soon as she reached her home out in the country, Jack drove up behind her car and got out. He was all smiles and hurried to take her in his arms, and kissed her like he was the happiest man on earth. "Where are the kids?"

"They're with Shannon right now. She and Chase run the Pinyon Pines Resort cabins at Lake Buchanon. Her mate is a part-time deputy sheriff also and they have two-year-old twins of their own. She's taking them swimming in the lake. I was supposed to meet them shortly. I was delayed and then here you are."

"Do we have time for..." He raised his brows, his arms wrapped around her.

She couldn't resist him. She'd never been able to. "If we make it quick. I don't want her to have to take care of them for long. So what's your news?" She took his hand and led him inside.

He scooped her up and took her into the hall. He didn't know the layout of the house and paused.

"My bedroom is first on the right."

"Okay, I have good news and not the greatest." He stalked toward the bedroom, kissing her forehead. "I was hired on with the CSF. I arrived early, arranged for an interview, and met with the director. Chuck was eager to have me work for them, but—"

"You have to train out of White Bear Lake first."

"Yeah. So I had to discuss it with you." He set her down on the king-size bed, the dark pine frame complimenting the ivory and pale blue and pink wedding quilt made by her grandmother. Pictures of her aunt, the kids, and Dottie's parents and grandparents filled the walls. But he smiled when he saw the one that she'd taken of him holding the kids' hands at the Renaissance fair. She had printed and framed it to include him with the collection of family photos.

His attention returned to her. She couldn't believe he'd ask her opinion about taking the job, but then again, she supposed if he really wanted to be with her, he wanted her to have a say in it. "What do you want to do?"

He held her hand. "I want to marry you, Dottie. In all the years I've been away, I've only thought of getting back together with you. Hell, I love you. I knew it from the moment I saw you again at the airport."

She loved him right back, her eyes filling with tears with heartfelt emotion. After the disastrous relationship with the boyfriend that she'd broken up with before she'd met Jack, and her marriage to Jeffrey, she didn't think she would ever meet someone who would be right for her. But not only for her. She had her children to think of. Who better to be their father than the man she'd fallen in love with, who was already their biological father, and had really shown how much he cared about them in the couple of weeks they'd been together.

"I'd love working for the CSF. I don't want to be separated from you for that long—ten to twelve months, Chuck said. I don't want to uproot you and the kids from here either." Jack ran his hands through his hair, and in that instant, he looked frustrated like he didn't know what to do exactly.

She didn't imagine Jack was ever indecisive about anything. At least as long as they'd known each other, he hadn't been. He acted as though he wanted to be with her and the kids, but he didn't want to lose her over the separation.

She took his hand and pulled him down to sit on the bed next to her. "What brand of condoms do you use?"

Jack frowned at her, probably wondering why she didn't say something about loving him or marrying him, or something more that suited the conversation. But she couldn't delay telling him about the pregnancy test.

"Are you ready to be a daddy again?" She didn't know how he'd take the news. This time, she wasn't going to wait to tell him what he was in for.

His jaw dropped. And then he smiled. "Hell. Yeah." He rubbed her shoulders, his eyes dark and intrigued, yet he looked amazed that he was going to be a father again, when he probably wasn't used to being one yet.

"I was afraid you wouldn't welcome the news."

He leaned down and kissed her. "Of course I welcome the news. I'm thrilled. When do we get married? Or...should I ask, will you marry me?"

She laughed. "I thought you'd never ask. And yes!"

They kissed to seal the bargain and he rubbed her back, hugging her soundly. He'd thought of getting the kids involved in the marriage proposal, but he hadn't wanted to wait any longer. Especially when she was pregnant with his child again.

"I'd say just keep the marriage simple, but I can't. All my friends are going to want to take part in it and your family and mine too. So it's not going to be easy to have something just quick and convenient."

"What if we have a justice of the peace marry us, and then we can have the big wedding sometime after that, when everyone can plan to be there. You can let your family and friends know we're getting married, and then take it from there."

"Before I tell everyone I'm pregnant."

"Yeah. My folks and my sister are going to be elated." He kissed her again. "Do you want to wait on this, and we can find out what we need to do to get married first?"

"Are you kidding? No. I haven't seen you in three months, and I'm not delaying this for any reason."

Dottie had been anticipating being with Jack all these months and she couldn't believe he was really here, undressing her, kissing her, making her blood sizzle. Just like she was kissing him and removing his clothes, smelling his musky, spicy scent that told her he was just as eagerly needing this as she was. She slid her hands over his muscular arms, loving the feel of him, the way his kisses turned from cherished to molten hot. The way his pheromones and hers

112

incited each other's to take this all the way.

He yanked the covers aside, and she laid against the bed while he continued kissing her.

She kissed him without reserve, her hands stroking his back as his naked body slid against hers, his hand sliding down her thigh in a sensual caress. She decided right then and there, she was following him wherever he went—to White Bear Lake if he had to train there, or even into the army. It didn't matter. She wanted to be with him and he needed to be with her and the kids. Just as much as the kids needed to be with their daddy.

He tangled his tongue with hers. His stiffened cock rubbed up against her mound as he kissed her throat and then her breast bone. He gently suckled a nipple, his hand lightly caressing the other breast. To her surprise, he moved down further and kissed her small baby bump. She smiled down at him and ran her hands over his hair. This was a new experience for him, and for her.

That was another reason to be with him for now. She needed the intimacy and time to be close like this until the baby was born.

He stroked her swollen nub, already primed and eager for his touch. She shuddered with pent-up need and desire.

The flicker of the stirrings of a climax quickly flared into a full-blown orgasm and she disintegrated into a million pieces.

***

Jack surged forward, pushing into her, deepening until he was snug in her wet heat. He belonged with her and he was seriously considering taking any job he could get in town. Maybe someone needed a security guard. Anything that would keep him in Yuma Town with Dottie and the twins. He continued to thrust deeply, thinking briefly about the brand new condoms he'd bought that were still in his pants pocket, and recalling she was already pregnant.

He felt the end coming, just as she cried out with release again, and he growled with contentment as his own climax hit. For a long moment, he just lay there with her, then remembering the baby, he rolled off Dottie and pulled her against his chest to cuddle. He loved this time with her, the aftermath of lovemaking, the feeling of release and gratification. "You are beautiful and I love you," he whispered against her hair.

"You are too, and I love you right back," Dottie said, snuggling comfortably against him.

After making love, they cuddled. Jack reached over to get his phone off the side table. "I'm going to check and see how we go about getting married fast."

"No Las Vegas wedding."

He smiled. "Wouldn't think of it." He didn't know why he hadn't looked into the procedure to marry Dottie prior to coming here. Not that he hadn't been swamped with work and trying to get out-processed at the end, and trying to line up the job with the CSF, so he could come home to Dottie and the kids. He wanted to see Jeff and Trish too. If they could take care of the marriage license application right away, he wanted to do that first, and then pick up the kids.

He did a couple of searches and said, "Okay, good, we can apply for the marriage license online. Then we need to drive to Loveland to pick up the marriage license at the Clerk and Recorder's Office to sign it and then get the judge to marry us." He smiled. "They say here that if you get it at the Loveland Larimer County Clerk and Recorder's Office, your marriage will have 'The Sweetheart City' included."

She laughed. "Okay, sounds good."

"We can be married by a judge, retired judge, magistrate, clergy, or do it on our own. The person solemnizing the marriage just completes the certificate and sends it in to the Larimer County Clerk and Recorder's Office and we're legally married. No blood test, no residency requirements, no waiting." He pulled up the application.

She loved how he jumped right in with both feet, no hesitation. But what were they going to do about his job situation? Still, she was glad they were getting married. They would make everything else work out however they could.

"Who do you think we should have certify that we're married? Wait, your boss. He's the sheriff. Yeah, that would be perfect. No one would doubt the validity of the marriage license then."

"Uh, yeah, I guess."

"It could be someone else if you prefer. From what this says, anyone will do."

"I think Dan would be perfect. I'll call Shannon and tell her we have to run to Loveland to take care of this business. I might as well get the ball rolling."

"Okay, what do you want me to do?"

She looked at his hunky nakedness and smiled. "Maybe get dressed?"

He laughed, then hurried to get dressed. "You want to make the rest of the calls in the car?"

"Sure. That will give me a chance to make all the arrangements on the way there, and let everyone know what's happening." She finished getting dressed and called

Shannon first to make sure it was okay with her that she was going to leave Trish and Jeff there for so long. Then again, they could take them with them. "Do you want to take the kids with us?"

"Either way is fine with me. I'll leave it up to you. I'm going to call Chuck Warner and see if there's any way he can give us a break and let me be here after maybe a month of training. Or maybe I should just ask Dan if I could work as a part-time deputy until I can work out something else."

"I'll see if Shannon can take care of the kids first, and then if not, we'll take them with us. As to the situation with the job, let's just get this taken care of first."

"You do love me, don't you?" Jack asked, pulling her in for a hug.

"Are you kidding? I thought that was rather obvious." She smiled up at him. "Yeah, Jack, I love you. I was so afraid the business between us was a case of rebound in the beginning. What we have is so much more." She kissed him soundly. Then she reluctantly pulled away so she could call Shannon, as Jack led her out to the car. "Hey, Shannon, I'm not going to make it to swim with you and the kids. Would you mind terribly taking care of them for about five or six hours?"

"I would love to keep them. I have to know if this is good news concerning Jack."

Dottie climbed into the car and Jack shut her door for her. "Yeah. We're going to Loveland to get a marriage license."

Silence.

Jack got behind the steering wheel and drove down the driveway and then onto the country road.

"I'm going to ask Dan if he'll sign the paperwork. If he's unable to, maybe you could do it? Or Chase?"

"Are you sure you're not jumping into this too quickly? Maybe you should get to know him better."

"No, he's the one. He's always been the one. I just couldn't see it because of his military obligation."

"What about his work situation?"

Jack turned and drove up the main road to Loveland.

"We'll figure out something. If I have to, I'll move with him to White Bear Lake," Dottie said to Shannon over the phone.

"In Minnesota? No way. I'll ask Chase to talk to Dan about a position here in Yuma Town as a deputy sheriff if the CSF can't relax their policy concerning where Jack is trained."

Dottie wasn't sure if Dan would want Jack working for

him. She glanced out the window at the pines they were passing by, thinking of running with Jack and the kids in this area, glad he was finally here.

"But yeah, I'll sign the paperwork. Ask Dan first though. He's your boss, and you've been friends for so long, I wouldn't exclude him. We're still going to do the wedding, right? You can't escape that."

Dottie smiled. "Yes, we want to. We want to get married right away, just in case we do have to be separated for a while." Especially with Dottie being pregnant again! She'd mention it only after she and Jack were married though. A few hours wouldn't make much of a difference.

"Okay, well, we're good here. Get something to eat in Loveland, enjoy yourselves before you're an old married couple. You already have the kids."

Dottie laughed. Little did Shannon or anyone else but the doctor know… Then she and Shannon ended the phone call and she punched in Dan's number. "I'm getting married to Jack Barrington. Will you fill out the paperwork and sign it for us?" she hurried to say.

"Hell, Dottie. You just met the guy."

"I've known him for some time. He's right for me. He's the father of my kids." She knew Jack would assume her boss wasn't really backing this marriage. He had to understand that her friends only wanted the best for her. They hadn't even met Jack yet. They didn't really know him at all.

"For what it's worth, I think you should wait. He's here now, right? So just...date for a while. He can stay at the cabins. Get to know you again. And the kids. Give it some time. I understand he's going to White Bear Lake to train to be a CSF agent, and then when he's finished, after a year, you can see if he's still the one for you. That will give you time to see the matter more clearly," Dan said.

"You know, I fantasized that maybe you and I could be together." She needed to let Jack know that though she hadn't had relations with another man other than her rotten husband, she hadn't really believed she'd see Jack again. That he would have stayed in the service and made it a career.

Jack glanced at her.

"But it seems I'm not the only one who has secrets, Dan."

"You mean about your kids and who the father is?"

And that she had another on the way! "Yeah, so what's your secret?"

"I've never known you to be this impulsive. You always think things through." Dan avoided the question.

She didn't think anyone else knew what was going on with Dan, except maybe Leyton. There was some kind of unspoken communication going on between them. He wouldn't enlighten her one way or another.

"I've been thinking about this since I saw Jack in Missouri. I've been corresponding with him daily. It's done. We're getting married. Do you want to sign our marriage license? Or do I get Shannon or Chase to do it?"

"So just like that? He doesn't even have the decency to marry you so you can celebrate with your friends and family?"

She let her breath out in exasperation. "That will come next. We want this done before he has to leave for that CSF training, unless you can use another deputy sheriff."

Dan didn't jump in and tell her he would hire him.

"I know you're concerned about me, but I know what I'm doing...this time around." Dottie didn't want anyone thinking they needed to intervene on her behalf this time. Yes, she'd made a horrible mistake marrying Jeffrey. Jack wasn't anything like him.

"I checked further into his background. So did Leyton and Chuck. Well, because he wanted to work with them. He's clean," Dan said.

She fought the urge to hang up on Dan! She had to remind herself that he and the others were trying to protect her from marrying the wrong kind of guy again. But this was not the same as before. And Jack was the children's father. "Dan, yes, or no?"

"If you are set on this course."

"I am."

"All right. When?"

"We're on our way to Loveland to get the marriage license, and we'll be back in about four and a half hours from now."

"You know where to find me."

"Thanks, Dan. See you later." Though from the grouchy way Dan had talked, she was thinking that maybe she should just have Shannon do the honors.

When she ended the call, Jack cleared his throat. "Do you want to wait a bit? Let your friends get to know me first?"

"No. Dan and the others just know how devastated I was with my first marriage and the trouble Jeffrey caused when he returned. They'll come around." Her phone rang and she saw the call was from Deputy Sheriff Stryker Hill.

Either Shannon or Dan must have already told him what was up. Or Shannon had told her deputy sheriff husband,

Chase, and he had told Stryker. News really got around fast in the cougar town.

"Hey, you've probably heard I'm getting married. Just a quick one and then a fancier one later when we can invite everyone."

"Are you sure about this, Dottie? Last time—"

"Last time, my husband was a liar and an arms' dealer. Jack is the father of my kids and a good guy. Ask Dan. He even had him investigated. No skeletons in his closet, okay? I know his family—his mom, Lisa, his dad, John, and his sister, Roberta. They love me and the kids. I'm fine. Just be happy for me. All right? I'll talk to you later. Bye." She ended the call. She didn't need all the negativity about this right now. She only wanted to feel good about this. She was certain everything would work out. By the time they returned, she figured the whole town would know about it.

She sat in silence for a few minutes, Jack being just as quiet, then he said, "Maybe you might like to join me in White Bear Lake for a while so we can be a family until I can get a job in Yuma Town. By then, your friends would realize we're staying together. And that we love each other. That we're good together. All of us."

"If the kids and I move to a new area and you're off

123

training or working somewhere else, I won't have cougar friends to talk to. And I want Kate to deliver the baby. I'm close to everyone here. I isolated myself after Jeffrey took off and left me to take care of the babies on my own. I don't want to be isolated like that again. But that said, I don't want to be separated from you again. The kids need to get to know you. We'll follow you wherever you end up and my friends will come around eventually." She just hoped they would sooner than later.

"But you need the support system from the cougars of Yuma Town. I have no idea what my schedule might be like. I might be gone for weeks at a time. I've already decided that I'll just take any job I can in Yuma Town. Later, maybe there will be other job options. But for now, I want to be with you and the kids. That way you'll still have your friends whom you can confide in, and your local doctor to see that everything's progressing fine with the baby."

"Thank you, Jack." But she had made up her mind. If he didn't find a job he liked, she wasn't going to let him sacrifice his career. He could end up hating the job, and resenting her and the kids. "We'll see what happens."

"When will you learn if it's a girl or a boy?"

"Next month. Do you want to know?"

"I do. I'm not much for surprises."

She laughed at that.

"Well, I mean about the sex of the child. Then we can decide on a theme for the nursery."

She couldn't believe he'd even be interested in the room decorations. She loved him.

Her cell rang and she saw the call was from Kate. "Congrats on getting married. Let us all know what you want to do for a wedding!"

"I want it to be low key. I've already been married once and with having two kids and another on the way, it seems silly to have a really big wedding."

"Everyone will want to come."

"Of course. But just keep the pregnancy secret until I announce it later, once we're married. Dan's going to sign the paperwork on the marriage certificate."

Kate was quiet.

"You didn't already tell anyone, did you?" Dottie had the sinking feeling she had.

"Dan saw your car at the clinic earlier. He called to tell me you were planning to marry Jack and I thought you had told him you were pregnant, because he's your boss and you'll need to take off time from work when the baby is due.

I'm sorry, Dottie. I really thought you'd told him. No wonder he didn't say anything."

Dottie groaned. "I haven't told anyone about the pregnancy. Not even my family. Just you and Jack."

"I'm so sorry. I'll call him right back and tell him not to say anything to anyone."

"Thanks. But it's probably too late." A siren wailed behind them, and Dottie glanced back to see that it was Dan's sheriff's car. "Omigod, don't bother. He's chasing us down, fixing to arrest someone, by the looks of it."

"Oh, no, I'm so sorry. I'll call him anyway and tell him not to share with anyone."

"Good luck with that." Dottie knew it was too late for anything. She glanced back at the flashing lights as Jack pulled the car onto the shoulder of the road and waited. "I'm so sorry about all of this."

"Don't be," Jack said. "It's touching to see how much everyone cares for you. When I'm away on assignment, I'll know you're in good hands."

Dan got out of his car and walked to the driver's side, looking all official and sheriff-like.

CHAPTER 5

When Dan reached the car door, Jack rolled down his window.

"Tell me you're marrying him because you want to and not because he got you pregnant—again," Dan said, looking straight at Dottie, seated in the passenger seat on the other side of Jack, as if he wasn't sitting there.

"Dan, you have no authority to pull us over as if Jack disobeyed any traffic laws. You're abusing your power." She was furious with him. Even though she understood he was concerned for her, she knew Jack was the right one for her.

"Well, are you?" Dan asked, ignoring the truth of the matter.

"No! I'm marrying him because I want to. Because I love him. And because he loves me and the kids right back. If you want to follow us into Loveland and marry us right there, then do so. Or we can drop by Tracey's parents' home, and have one of them sign off." She figured if push came to shove, they could just have them sign off on it because they lived right there in Loveland too and then Dottie and Jack could drop the paperwork off at the courthouse and it would be done. "It's your choice. Be a part of this, or don't."

"We haven't met," Jack said, offering his hand to Dan. He was just as serious, not cowing to Dan, but congenial. "I served in the same unit as you, from what I understand. Good to meet you. I'll do right by Dottie. I would have done so a long time ago if she hadn't been so adverse to me marrying her when I was on active duty."

Dan finally shook Jack's hand, and Dottie let out a relieved breath. "She has a lot of friends here. We don't want to see her leave town to join you. If Chuck Warner can't see fit to have you transferred to Leyton's unit at an early enough date, I'll take you on as my deputy. But you'll need training."

Jack smiled and nodded. "Thank you." He reached over and rubbed Dottie's shoulder. "I'd really like to stay with Dottie and the kids and be here when she has the baby."

Dan gave him a stern look. "Whose fault is that?"

"Dan—" Dottie wasn't about to have Jack take the

blame. It was none of anyone's business.

"Like Dottie said, you can join us and get the paperwork signed, or we can return here, or just have someone else do it. She would love to have you do the honors. It's your choice," Jack said, not taking any of Dan's guff.

"I'll follow you. If I get a call, I may have to take it. I'm still on duty."

Dottie was so thankful that Dan was going to do it.

"Thanks." Jack waited for Dan to return to his car, then once Dan turned off his lights, Jack pulled back onto the road. "Well, hell, now I have two job offers."

"Which would you rather do?"

"Work for your boss who hates me? Or work for Chuck and hope he frees me to work in Yuma Town under Leyton sooner than later?" Then Jack got a call on his Bluetooth, and he suspected it might be from one of the Yuma Town cougars that were upset with him too. But it was Chuck, head of the CSF.

"Hey, Dan just called me and said he offered you a job if I didn't allow you to work closer to home. Seems Dottie's pregnant again."

Dottie's jaw dropped. The whole world was going to know before her own aunt even did!

"I like your resume, liked your interview, and was looking forward to having you work for me. But I understand your need to work closer to home."

Dottie was afraid that meant he was going to withdraw the offer to have Jack work as a CSF agent when she really thought Jack would prefer that.

"I talked briefly with Leyton. He said he'd train you, just so you'd be able to stay in Yuma Town. He hasn't ever trained a new agent before. But he's one of my best. If you think you can work with him, then that's what we'll do."

Jack smiled. "Hell, yeah, thanks so much, Mr. Warner. That will be perfect."

"But you'll need to be focused on the job."

"Absolutely." Jack looked thrilled.

And Dottie was thrilled too. She couldn't believe how everyone had pulled together to make this happen. Now she was glad the news of her pregnancy had spread like wildfire.

"Okay, well, I'll let you go, and you can always take some more training with me later."

"Okay, good deal. Thanks, sir."

"Just call me Chuck. No formalities. We all just want to take down the bad guys and keep the good guys safe."

"Thanks, Chuck. You don't know how much I appreciate

this."

"I think I have an inkling. Good luck. I'll check on your progress with the job later."

"That's what you really wanted to do, wasn't it?" Dottie asked Jack when they ended the call.

"Yeah. I think I can do a lot of good with taking down rogue cougars. If things get slow, I can even help Dan out. But I think for now, I'd love being a CSF agent working for Leyton."

"You're sure you don't mind leaving the service?"

"Are you kidding? Not when I have a family to be with."

"Speaking of which, we need to let our families know all the news."

"I can call your aunt," he said, smiling.

"She'll be thrilled."

When they called Aunt Emily, she was ecstatic.

"I know you hate flying," Dottie said. "But maybe you can ride with Jack's parents and sister?"

"I'll do that. Just let me know when the wedding will take place. Oh, I'm so happy for the two of you, though I have to admit I'm a bit jealous he asked you and not me."

Dottie and Jack laughed.

"If she hadn't said yes..." Jack laughed again.

"Do you know what the baby is going to be yet? I have to get ready for this. I'm so excited."

"Not yet, Aunt Emily. We'll let you know as soon as we do."

They called his family next and they said they'd bring Aunt Emily along with them. "I probably shouldn't ask this, son, but...you do know about birth control, or had you planned this?"

Jack smiled at Dottie. She raised her brows slightly.

"Brand new condoms both times. Maybe I should have used a generic brand. Hell, I don't know."

"Dad," Roberta scolded in the background.

"Just checking," John said. "In all honesty, we're glad the two of you are getting together for good. Just let us know the date."

Dottie had to take calls all the rest of the way to Loveland from all her lady friends, wanting to wish her well, and asking her when the baby was due. She guessed Kate hadn't told Dan that part or everyone would have known everything.

Then Leyton called Jack, and welcomed him to the CSF. "I hear you need to be located near family for the training."

"Yeah, thanks, Leyton, for agreeing to train me."

"We work long hours, sometimes weeks away from home."

"I completely understand. At least for the time being, it will be a lot better than training away from home for nearly a year."

"Okay, I know you're in the process of getting hitched right now, but let me know when you can start training too, and we'll get started."

"Thanks. Will do."

When they ended the call, Dottie said, "You might as well get started right away, if you can. That way you'll get the training done, and probably have more time for when the baby is actually due. In the meantime, we can figure out the wedding date, and I'm sure Leyton will let you off for that. Well, and he'll attend the wedding with his mate too, Jack."

"Sounds like a good plan to me."

They parked at the office where they had to get the paperwork, and Dan looked nice and official in his uniform, though Dottie thought it looked a little like they were under arrest.

He seemed to have finally gotten used to the idea, a little, that she was both marrying Jack and having another of his babies, for which she was glad. She loved everyone in

Yuma Town. She loved Jack too, and she wanted everyone to love him as much. Or...at least like him.

Dan said to Jack, "Chuck must have really wanted you to work on his team. He told me that in no way were you working for me."

"If you ever need a hand, I'll be there for you," Jack said, serious as could be.

Dan smiled a little at him. She hoped Jack hadn't made a mistake in offering.

After they signed the paperwork and Dottie and Jack were truly married, which she was thrilled with, and from the adoring expression her mate was wearing, he felt the same way too, Dan congratulated them, shaking Jack's hand. "Don't get in any trouble now." He gave Dottie a hug. "I'll see you on Monday, correct?"

"Of course. Thanks, Dan, for everything."

Then Dan tipped his hat and took off.

Dottie received a text from Shannon saying they were keeping Trish and Jeff overnight so Dottie and Jack could have their "newlywed" night alone together. She thought the world of her and Chase.

"Should we just get a hotel room here?" Jack asked.

"No. My home is yours now too. I want to be home with

you." She'd thought of nothing else for three months. "I'll fix us a steak dinner when we get home. If you don't mind, on the drive there, I'll make wedding arrangements for two weeks from today."

"Sounds good to me, Mrs. Barrington. And I want you to know whatever you want to do about work is fine with me. But if you'd like to stay home with the kids, I can support us so you're able to."

"Thanks. I was thinking about that. Arranging for care for the twins is expensive, and I hate imposing on friends if I'm not paying them. Besides, I'd like to be a full-time mother again, like I was when the twins were born."

When they arrived home, she showed him the pictures that the kids had made, welcoming him home. They really touched him, and he was all for going to Shannon and Chase's place and picking them up.

"We won't have a lot of time where we're free to see each other like this when Jeff and Trish are home and we're both off from work." She took his hand and led him into the bedroom. "And we're newlyweds, besides."

CHAPTER 6

The next morning, Jack's phone rang and he was surprised to see Leyton was calling him on Saturday. "Ready to start your training?"

Right this minute? No. Jack was still enjoying the afterglow of making love to his lovely wife.

"Yeah, sure." Jack didn't want to let on to his brand new boss that he wanted to stay with Dottie a while longer this morning. Well, all weekend, truth be told.

"Meet me at the office. Travis MacKay, my partner, is coming with us. We'll make sure you have a firearm and tell Dottie we might be gone for a few days."

Jack hated that. Sure, it was better than being gone for months, but he'd wanted to see the kids before he had to take off. He'd been really looking forward to it.

"Okay. Any idea when we're coming back?"

"Think of this like an army mission. You have no idea when it will be accomplished, sooner than later, you hope. Whoever knows."

Training meant schedules, so either this wasn't a training mission, or Leyton wasn't sure how much Jack needed to get with the program. Or, Leyton was testing him to see if he could handle uncertainty. Jack had been through all that in the army, so he knew just fine how to deal with it, but Leyton wouldn't know that until he witnessed it firsthand.

"I'll let Dottie know and then I'll be right over."

"Grab some breakfast, pack a bag, and meet us in an hour. Then we'll be on our way."

"Will do."

Leyton gave him the address. Jack ended the call and pulled Dottie into his arms.

"Leyton wants you to start training *today*?"

"Yeah. And he said he has no idea when we'll be returning. You know what I think? He has a real mission to go on, and he wants me to get my feet wet."

Dottie rubbed his arm, not looking happy about it.

He shrugged. "It's a job."

"Yeah, I know. I just...I just hoped we'd have the weekend together. You, me, and the kids."

"Me too. But if we can wrap this up quickly, we'll be done and home before you know it."

She sighed. "Okay, let me start breakfast while you're getting packed."

They both got out of bed and she threw on a pair of sweats and headed out of the room while he took a quick shower, wishing he was soaping up Dottie too.

Then they had breakfast, and he headed out. "I'll let you know whatever I can, when I can."

"Okay. Love you."

He gave her a warm hug and a hotter kiss, then let out his breath. "Hell, this better be worth it."

She laughed. "I'm sure you'll be home soon."

He sure hoped so as he headed over to the house where Leyton and Travis had set up the CSF office. It was also a hangout/safe-house for fellow CSF agents if they needed a place to stay while they were in the area. It was a two-story white house with a picket fence, just like many of the homes in the neighborhood.

Travis MacKay and Leyton Hill greeted him, congratulating him on the marriage, and the new baby.

Leyton had short, dark brown hair and a scruffy beard, whereas Travis was clean-shaven, his hair just as short, but the color was much darker. Both were six-feet tall, muscular, looking like they worked out and would make a good team.

Travis gave him a Glock and ammo. Leyton showed Jack the map of the locations where they were headed, and they gave him some of the background on the case. It *wasn't* a training mission.

"We're going after the guy who was the third man involved in an attack on us at Pine Ridge Gold Mine near Hal and Tracey Haverton's horse ranch. He managed to escape prosecution—which, in our line of work as CSF agents, often means taking the bad guys down permanently—and we've only just now received word that he's back in the area. The other two cougars who were involved in the crimes are dead. Your mate's ex-husband was one of the men. The third guy's name is Bishop Adkins and he's just as dirty as Jeffrey Brown and the other guy, Curly Joe. Like the other two, Bishop is a wily, rogue cougar shifter. He's picked up a new partner. The guy was just released from jail. A man named Hellion Crichton."

"Ah, hell."

Travis and Leyton carried their gear out to his black

Suburban. "You know the guy?" Leyton asked.

"Yeah. I dated his sister back in Missouri. We'd been engaged to be married and I learned she was cheating on me and broke it off. Hellion attacked me when I was running as a cougar with Dottie. The guy's a habitual criminal. Assault, battery, attempted murder, if you count him trying to shoot me."

"You got that right. And Bishop is on the same par as him. They were incarcerated together some time back," Leyton said as Jack put his bag in Leyton's vehicle.

"I take it this isn't exactly a training exercise," Jack said, not that he figured he needed a lot of classroom training.

"We do on-the-job training. Every situation is different for us. Isn't that right, Travis?"

"I'll say. One time I'm saving Leyton's life, the next, he's saving mine. Then my mate is saving mine, and I was saving Chet Kensington's, another CSF agent with the force. We never know what we'll be facing."

"Any problem with that?" Leyton asked as he got in to drive.

"Nope. I'm good with thinking on my feet and improvising."

"Good. That's what we'd read in your paperwork. And

that's the kind of agents we need. We certainly can't rely on someone who has to take all of his guidance from us, just in case we're...a bit tied up at the time." Leyton smiled. "Besides, I'd hate to have to tell Dottie that we just killed her brand new mate. By the way, all of us guys are wondering, did you plan to have more kids?"

Jack laughed. "No. That just happened. Leaky condoms, I guess."

Leyton chuckled and shook his head.

"I heard Hal used the same brand," Travis said.

Jack laughed. "I guess this mission is all hush-hush, as far as telling the wives."

"No. You can tell Dottie what you feel you need to. I didn't want to mention it to you when you were at your house in the event you didn't want her to know you were going on a live mission your first time out."

"Because she was afraid of me fighting in a war if I had to and not returning?"

"Exactly."

Jack really wasn't certain how she'd take the news. But he wasn't going to keep secrets from her.

"So tell us what you know about Hellion, since you've had a personal run-in with him. His strengths, weaknesses.

All we know about him is what we learned from police reports." Travis handed pictures of the men in their human form back to Jack. Bishop was a narrow-eyed, swarthy, non-smiling little guy. Hellion was big, bulky, mean-looking as ever.

"Hellion's got a real mean streak. He likes to act tough, but it's not all an act either."

"For example?" Travis asked.

"Threatening people he had some run-in with. One time he came with us, his sister and me, to a movie. We were still engaged at the time. She wanted to take him. I said sure, because I'm close to my family, and I didn't mind getting to know her brother better. He threw candy wrappers out in the parking lot, and someone gave him grief for littering. Hellion got in his face and told the man if he didn't like it, pick it up himself. The other man backed down. Gigi laughed, which gave me the impression she wasn't in the least bit bothered by her brother's belligerent behavior."

"What did you do?" Leyton asked.

"Told Hellion the man was right. Only a slob would dump his trash all over. And if anyone was trying to collect evidence on him, his fingerprints would be all over it. The law enforcement official wouldn't even need a warrant. The trash would be public property at that point. I figured Hellion would have been jumping down my throat next, but he just stared at me with the most hellish look. Then he smiled a little, if his sneer could be called a smile, and grabbed up the trash. He said, 'Yeah, you never know what the Feds are going to pin on you.' Then he gave the other man a caustic look, but he was already headed for the ticket booth. Anyway, I saw what Hellion was like. You don't tell him anything he doesn't want to hear or he goes ballistic. When he came after Dottie and me on the run a few weeks after I'd broken off my engagement with Gigi, I knew he was really bad news. A real psycho. Then, after robbing a convenience store, he came after me at my apartment with a loaded gun. I helped put him away and I'm sure he hates me even more for it."

"He's going to love you when we take him down again," Travis said.

"Only this time, it's going to be permanent," Leyton said. "We're just damn lucky neither of the men shifted into their cougars on jail time. It's hard enough dealing with not liking something if you have a volatile temper when you could just shift and take care of the threat in your cougar coat. What about Bishop? Know anything about him?" Leyton asked.

"Nope. Never heard of him. Never saw him before either. Do you have any pictures of Bishop as a cougar?"

"No. We'll have to wing it. We'll be staying at a cabin a few hours from Yuma Town and running as cougars for a while. I've been out there before, chasing down his old partner. You wouldn't happen to have known him in the army, would you?"

"By the name of Jeffrey Brown? No, not that I recall."

"He was Bart Smith in the army. Then when he first got out, he changed his name to Butch Sanders. When he met Dottie, he was Jeffrey Brown."

"What was his real name, do you know?" Jack asked.

"Zylen Wilson Miller. That's the name he was born with."

Jack was glad the man's real name hadn't been Jeffrey since Dottie's and Jack's son was named Jeff. Which, meant as far as he was concerned, Dottie had named their son after her uncle and Jack's middle name, Alexander.

"He tried to kill me while we were under enemy fire. He used an enemy's rifle to make it look like the enemy had shot me. Then he returned to his unit, and since no one had witnessed the incident but me, it was my word against his. He left the service after that, honorably discharged, and then was on a police force for a while. But he was a dirty cop. When he got out, I was already with the CSF and tracked him down. He was a priority mission for us," Leyton said.

"Yeah, he was bad news. Just as much as the other two men he was with," Travis said.

"I'm glad you took him down. And that he didn't get to Dottie and the kids."

"So how did you feel about learning you were a dad with twins?" Leyton asked.

"Hell, I was shocked, just like any single man would be who didn't know he'd fathered any kids. I didn't even know she had any. Or that she'd been married."

"So once you picked yourself up off the floor?" Leyton asked, looking back over the seat at him.

"I was thrilled. Asked her aunt to see baby pictures. Jeff is the spitting image of me at that age. I can't tell you how that made me feel."

"Proud, I imagine. And protective," Travis said.

"Hell yeah. I've always loved Dottie, though I wasn't sure if she felt the same way about me and would want to make a go of it. Once I learned she had the twins, I hoped more than ever to convince her that she needed me in her life. Sounds kind of sappy, doesn't it?"

Leyton and Travis laughed.

"If we hadn't fallen into the same predicament, minus the kids, I might have thought so. But I feel the same way about Bridget," Travis said.

"Same with Kate and me," Leyton agreed.

"Okay, so we're staying at a cabin and you figure these guys are headed in that direction, or staying nearby?" Jack asked.

"Yeah, we had another man on the job. Chet tracked them to this area and the thing of it was, this is where I'd tracked one of their cohorts before, Butch, as I knew him. Chuck recalled Chet and told him he needed him in Wyoming on another case. He also didn't want him out here on his own, like I was last time."

"Hell, that was the best thing that ever happened to you," Travis said. "You kidnapped Kate from her clinic and made a camping trip out of it."

Jack wondered what that was all about.

"And you were all tied up nice and pretty like a Christmas package, until Bridget rescued you," Leyton said to Travis.

"Yeah, that was the best thing that ever happened to me."

Jack smiled. "Hell, sounds like my relationship with Dottie's been rather boring."

"We're glad for that," Leyton said. "She's been through a lot. And she's not a highly trained operative like most of us are. She needs stability and a loving husband and father for the kids."

"I plan to be that." Jack further pondered what Leyton had told him about the guys returning to the area. "So have you figured out why these guys keep coming here? It seems to me if we knew why, we might be able to get ahead of their moves. Also, I wonder why they'd come here when they know you realize that they keep returning here."

"They don't know that we're onto them. Only Butch was out this way. Hellion, as far as we know, has never been here. When we had trouble at the mine, the three men were there. But we lost track of Bishop. I suspect that Butch didn't tell Bishop that I chased him all over this area before I got shot and couldn't go after him for a while."

"But you're sure it's something out here?"

"I would think so," Leyton said. "I found a cache of weapons and destroyed it. They have a cabin too, they've been using. Same one as before."

"And they didn't smell your scent there?"

147

"We came back and cleaned up the place. He would never know we'd been there."

"How far is our cabin from theirs?"

"Five miles. Short jog in the park as cougars. Far enough away that we're not on top of them. We'll run over there tonight as cougars and see who all is there," Leyton said.

"So we can't have any fire at our cabin?" Jack asked.

"We'll be like regular campers. Fire, roasting Smore's. The works," Travis said. "Gotta have some fun on this job before all the biting and shooting, etcetera. If they did manage to snoop around here, we'd just take care of them then. No having to chase after them."

"So let's say we find the two men there, then what? We just take them down?" In the army, they had rules. Especially since it was a human run organization, whereas this one was cougar run and was responsible for eliminating cougars who were real trouble. Jack wasn't exactly sure what the rules were with this outfit. From the sounds of it, they didn't take prisoners. Didn't prosecute the men on their radar.

"Okay, yeah. For these guys? They're both attempted murderers. The one in your case. The other in ours. We eliminate them. If these guys were civilians, we'd turn them over to the police. We work with them, though they only know of us as a secretive government organization. We have badges and ID that gives us some authority." Travis pulled a package out of the console and handed it back to Jack. "Keep them in good health."

"I wondered how we did this. Okay, so let's say we kill them. Then what? Surely, we can't just bury them anywhere."

"Chuck will arrange for a cleanup crew. We'll wait until they get here. Or Dan and his men might take care of it," Leyton said.

"What if the perps have enlisted other men's help? People we don't have any record of?"

Leyton drove down a gravel road. "Case by case situation. They shoot at us, we take them out. They come to kill us with claws and teeth, we take them out. If they give up? We'll take them in. We'll need to learn what else they've been involved in. The two men who have already tried to kill us? They don't stand a chance. Anyone else, we'll give them the benefit, if they give up willingly before they try to kill us."

Jack hoped he didn't do anything wrong like let the bad guys go, or get his partners injured or killed. "How does the chain of command work? I know you're in charge of the office in Yuma Town. But you still seem to be working with Chuck, taking his lead."

"Yeah, we have our own office, and he's still overall head of the organization. We're expanding as we need to. If I'm out of the office on an assignment, you'll go through Travis. If both of us are gone and you need guidance, call Chuck. We do go on independent missions, especially if one of us is on vacation, or we're only after one guy and we think we can handle it. For the next year, or less, depending how adaptable you are, you'll be with me or Travis. Or Bridget. She's also CSF and good at what she does." Leyton pulled into a parking area next to a log cabin. "This is it. We'll unpack our bags and food, have some lunch, go exploring a bit, and then wait until it's closer to dusk. This is a recon mission. That means we wait to see who all is there. If no one is, we hang around to see if anyone shows up, sniff around the place, determine how long ago anyone was there. According to Chet, Bishop should have been there just a couple of days ago, if not more recently than that."

Jack was eager to get on the way. These guys knew when to take care of the mission best, but he didn't want to wait. He wanted to get this over with and get home to Dottie and the kids.

"Whatever you do, put Dottie and the kids out of your

thoughts," Leyton said, carrying in one of the ice chests.

Jack grabbed another. "Gotcha."

"It's hard to do sometimes. But we really want to keep you focused on the mission." Travis seized several bags of groceries.

"Will do." Jack really thought he could do that. Sure, he'd think of her, but he was good at compartmentalizing what he needed to do now and what he needed to do later.

Later that night after trekking the five miles to the cabin and seeing a light on, the first thought Jack had was Hellion could be in there. He immediately recalled the details of the last cougar fight and human altercation he'd had with him. What he hadn't expected was for Gigi to appear at the window.

CHAPTER 7

Dottie picked up the kids at Shannon's house that morning, afraid they'd be disappointed that they hadn't seen their daddy yet. "He had to work at his new job."

"You said he was coming home," Jeff said.

"He did. Then Leyton called him to come work on the new job. Daddy might be gone for a few days. We thought he would have the whole weekend with you kids. Leyton really needed him though."

"*We* really needed him." Trish crossed her arms in a huff.

Dottie smiled. "You know most of the guys, and Tracey and Bridget, take down bad guys or rescue good guys, right?"

Jeff and Trish nodded and she got them into the car and buckled them in.

"Well, Leyton and Travis had to ask Daddy for help. Sometimes they need more helpers to take down the *really* bad guys."

"So when's he coming home?" Jeff asked.

"We're not sure. Maybe a couple of days. I have to go back to work on Monday. I have the whole weekend off to take you swimming, or running as cougars, whatever you want to do."

Then she got a call from Ted Weekum. Apparently, besides being the foreman at the Haverton's ranch, he was on baby delivery announcement duty. "Tracey and Hal are at the clinic now. They said it's just early labor. Hal wants her to stay there until she has the babies because they live so far out. But Kate and Tracey said no."

Dottie laughed. She remembered feeling the very same way when she had the twins. Jeffrey hadn't been there for her either. Thankfully, Stryker had been on patrol that day and nearby, so he had taken her into the clinic.

"Let me know when it's for real. I'll be right over then." When she got off the phone with Ted, she told the kids, "Tracey should be having her babies soon."

"When can they play with us?" Trish asked.

"Well, you remember when Shannon's twins were

born? Sadie and Zoey are two now and it took them a while before they were old enough from the time they were born to when they could really play with you. But remember, as kittens, they will love to play with you. You just have to be careful with them." She loved that about their cat shifter half. Human babies took so long to grow up, and that affected how quickly they grew as cougars too. They were still easier to handle and could get around on their own more as cougar cubs though.

***

Jack couldn't believe that Gigi was at the cabin where Hellion and Bishop were supposed to be meeting up. Jack and his fellow cougar agents checked out the area as close to the cabin as they could without catching her eye. Cougars could see movement really well, so they had to stay out of her sight. They finally climbed into different trees and just watched to see if anyone else would show up. He smelled that Hellion had been here a couple of days ago. Jack had smelled another male also and he assumed it was Bishop's scent. Unless they had another villain working with them. Gigi's scent was there too, and really fresh. So it appeared she was the only one here right now.

He couldn't believe she'd be here. Was she up to no

good along with the rest of the men? Or just staying at the cabin on vacation? He suspected that if she didn't know about their illegal dealings, she wouldn't be here. Even though she hadn't seemed to care that her brother had tried to kill him, he still couldn't see her as someone who would commit violent crimes also.

For four hours, they watched the house and the surrounding area. Except for Gigi moving around in the lighted cabin, then finally settling down for the night and turning off all the lights, nothing else happened. Neither her brother nor Bishop showed up.

Leyton leapt down from his tree and Travis followed suit. Jack thought someone should continue to watch the cabin. What if the men showed up in the middle of the night? What if the perps left for some other destination, and the agents didn't have a clue where they'd gone to next?

Leyton and Travis waited for him. Jack wasn't budging. He belatedly realized he was probably defying an order to leave, in a cougar way. Leyton nodded at him, acknowledging he could stay, then both cougars raced off. After another hour or so passed, Jack fell asleep. Any little noise would wake him, so he figured he might as well get some sleep.

About an hour after that, he heard a car roll up on the

gravel road and park next to the cabin.

Jack watched a man get out as the interior car lights illuminated him. It wasn't either Bishop or Hellion. Then a light came on inside the cabin and another cast a shadowy illumination on the front porch. Gigi rushed outside in sweats and threw herself at the man. He grabbed her up and carried her into the house, then slammed the door. Apparently he was Gigi's lover. But was he one of Bishop and Hellion's partners or just Gigi's lover?

Maybe Hellion and Bishop had already cleared out of there.

The lights went out again, and that was the end of any activity. Though Jack kept an eye peeled the whole time.

Before dusk, Jack saw a cougar approaching his tree, and he recognized Travis. The cougar jumped into the tree. Jack shifted and told him that the woman in the cabin was Hellion's sister, and about the new man and that no one else had appeared. Jack shifted back into his cougar form, and Travis shifted to give him orders.

"Return to the cabin. Get some shut-eye. Tell Leyton the news and we'll take shifts."

Jack nodded, then leapt from the tree and headed back to the cabin.

When he arrived there, Leyton was fixing eggs and ham on the gas stove and making toast. Jack went to the bedroom, shifted, and dressed, then joined Leyton in the small kitchen, walking across the wooden floor, making them creak. If anyone broke in on them, they'd hear them before they reached the bedrooms.

Pine cabinets, a pine wooden table for four, pine paneled walls, even in the bedrooms, a large brown, rust, and green braided rug, and country chairs and loveseats gave the cabin a rustic appearance. The living room was comfortable, a screened-in porch with a view of the river right off that, and the bedroom windows looked off into the woods. Each of the beds sported patchwork quilts and Jack was thinking how much fun it could be if he and Dottie and the kids had a cabin of their own like this someday.

"So did anything happen?" Leyton served up the eggs and ham onto two green ceramic plates.

Jack told him about Gigi and the other man.

"Hell. So you know her better than any of us. Is she involved in their criminal activities?"

They sat down at the kitchen table and Jack salted his eggs. "I don't know. In the past when I was engaged to her, I would never have suspected it. Now? Maybe. What exactly did Chet say Hellion and Bishop were doing?"

"Just hanging out here. Chet wanted to stay. But the boss had another mission for him and in no way did he want one man out here on his own trying to take the two men down. Now, does it mean that the man with Gigi is also one of their partners in crime?"

"Maybe. She didn't have any qualms about her brother trying to kill me. Some of it was probably because she was angry I had ended the engagement, but still, it made me reconsider the kind of person she is. Tell me exactly what happened with Jeffrey, Bishop, the other guy, Curly Joe." Jack forked up some of his eggs.

"We told you about the mine and the stash of weapons we found," Leyton said.

"Right, so that's why they were in the area. But why did Jeffrey return to Yuma Town? He'd left when the kids were one and didn't return for all that time. Why plan to take Dottie and the kids hostage?"

Leyton finished up his eggs and ham, then served a couple of fresh cups of coffee. "We don't know. When he took Kate hostage, I came to her rescue. Supposedly, Jeff wanted to take Dottie and the twins from there. Move to a new location. As if he really wanted to be with them."

"I don't believe that, do you? Or did he think to use them as cover again? It doesn't make sense. He really didn't want the kids, did he? Knowing that they weren't even his, and that he hadn't supported them all those years."

"From what Dan told me, Jeffrey had never helped with them, even when he was living with them. He'd never acted like a father to them. So no, I can't see that he'd return for them because of some sense of pride in his kids, or wanting to be part of their lives all of a sudden. Not with the business he was in. He hadn't told Dottie where he'd gone or if he'd ever return. She was well rid of him when she divorced him."

"Okay, so if he thought to use her as a cover in Yuma Town before everyone knew what he was up to, that's easy to see. But dragging around an unwilling ex-wife and her kids somewhere else?"

"We considered he was desperate. I don't know. We need to find Bishop, make him talk and determine what was up with Jeffrey concerning Dottie and the kids."

"Sounds good. So then what's the deal between Dan and Dottie?" Jack buttered his toast and coated it with blackberry jam.

"Nothing that you need to be concerned about. Once she returned home from seeing her aunt, the kids were excited about their daddy coming home in three months, and Dottie explained how she'd kept the secret from you." Leyton shrugged. "Unless you didn't show up like you said you would, we knew this was where the relationship was headed. All the kids could talk about was you being a knight and taking them to the Renaissance fair, taking them on all the rides at the theme park, and taking them to see the animals at the zoo. We thought you had to be the real deal."

"Dan wasn't happy about us getting married."

"He's been protecting her and the kids from rotten asses like her ex-husband. We've all had our own issues. Chase lost his wife and child some years ago; Stryker and I learned we're twins, but different families raised us. Kate learned never to take a nap at her clinic. No telling who might break in. Tracey was always in the middle of a shoot-out, and Hal was always trying to keep her out of them."

"Tracey, the one who's pregnant with twins?"

"Yep. And Chase's mate, Shannon, was on the run and they all took her in. I wasn't here yet."

"And Dan?"

"He was trying to make sure Dottie didn't lose her house when her husband left."

"He likes the kids, right?"

"Sure."

"And Dottie?" Jack couldn't help feeling like the sheriff was more interested in Dottie than as just a friend and boss.

"We all like Dottie."

"So why didn't he marry her?" After Dan had pulled Jack over when he and Dottie were on their way to Loveland to get their marriage license, Jack felt like something more was going on between them. That and the fact that Dan had wanted her to delay marrying Jack. Leyton didn't answer him. "She wouldn't have objected to marrying her boss, would she have?"

Leyton took the dishes into the kitchen.

Jack studied him, knowing Leyton knew something about the situation, even if he was new to the area. Just off the top of his head, Jack came up with the most unbelievable scenario he could think of, given how Dan had acted toward Dottie, but it would be a good reason not to propose marriage to her.

"He's gay."

Leyton chuckled.

Jack really hadn't believed that was the case. Then he thought of another unreal notion that would stop someone from marrying a person he really cared about. "He's already married."

Leyton glanced at him, no smile, no laugh, and in that instant, Jack knew the truth. "It's a secret. Who all knows about it?"

"No one. I suggest you keep it to yourself."

"But *you* know."

"I was pushing him to tell me why he didn't—" Leyton quit talking abruptly as if he decided he'd said too much.

"Ask her to marry him? So they were dating?"

"Not really dating. It was really low key. He'd go over to have dinner with her sometimes. Nothing that would have gotten him in trouble with a wife."

"So where is his wife? And why keep her a secret from everyone?"

"I don't know. I didn't ask. He has his reasons for not telling anyone about his wife. Hell, she may be in prison. Or in a mental institution. How do I know? I just know that when he feels the time is right, he'll share the truth with us. Just like Dottie finally did by telling us about you and that you are the father of her children. I wouldn't worry about Dan. He can take care of himself. The kids and Dottie absolutely love you, which is obvious. When they came home from Missouri, all the kids could do was talk about you. Daily, for three whole months, they've been excited about seeing you."

"I missed seeing them."

"Which is all good. A few more days won't hurt. Dottie will be busy with all the women getting ready to celebrate the marriage and she'll still be working. We're all glad for them and for you. Hell, I don't know what I would have done if I had been separated from Kate as long as you were apart from Dottie, feeling as you do and just finding out I had a couple of twins. I would have been here in a heartbeat, if I could have been."

"We're very happy. I just didn't want to create hard feelings with Dan or anyone else."

"I'm sure that knowing you're good for Dottie and the kids, and sticking around long-term, that's all that matters to anyone."

They heard a growl outside the door. Jack and Leyton pulled their guns as Jack went to get the door. He should have waited for Leyton to give him guidance, since the agent was supposed to be the one training him. Jack was so used to being in charge as a captain in the army, his reactions were based on instinct.

He pulled the door open, stepping back out of the line of fire in case the cat lunged at him. It was Travis. The agent quickly shifted in the entryway and said, "They're all there."

They'd expected to be outnumbering them by one—two bad guys, three good guys. So this changed the dynamics a bit.

Still, Jack was confident they could take them down.

"Gigi, the woman who's there, is Jack's ex-fiancée," Leyton informed him.

"Yeah, he told me. Hope it won't cause a problem," Travis said, turning his attention to Jack, his expression telling him that he wasn't sure Jack could deal with this since one of the perps might be an old girlfriend.

"No problem. Everyone's armed and human, right?" Jack asked.

"Yeah. No telling how long they'll be there." Travis headed for his room and called out, "I got the license plate number. Easy. It's Hel1. He most likely figured he couldn't use Hell because it might be considered profane."

"The newcomer's vehicle was V9R319, Missouri plates, Ford truck," Jack said.

Leyton wrote down the tags and got on his phone. "Okay, I want Jack to be a cougar, you and I will go armed to the teeth, and bring along his pack with his clothes and gun."

"You want me to go now?" Jack asked, wanting to make

sure they didn't lose sight of these people while they were talking.

"Yeah. Stay out of sight until we arrive."

"Gotcha." Jack stripped and shifted.

"No heroics," Leyton said. "If they leave before we get there, let them. Dottie would never forgive me if you got yourself killed on your first training mission." Leyton paused and spoke into the phone, "Hey, boss, here are the license plates of Hellion's vehicle and some newcomer. We're off to try and take them down." He paused. "Four, one of them is Jack's ex-fiancée." Leyton glanced at Jack. "He's good."

Jack nodded, then headed out. He never knew what would happen on an army mission—even when they were just conducting training. But he knew to be careful. He wasn't a Lone Ranger. In a case like this, he waited for backup. Unless the bad guys had taken someone hostage and were threatening to kill the person. That was different. Then he would take risks. He thought he could do whatever he needed to concerning Gigi if the time came. Did he want to kill her? No. If she tried to kill him or his fellow agents, and he didn't have a choice, he'd do what he had to do.

He was out the door in a flash, racing to reach the cabin so that he could observe what was going on. He hoped this went down well for the team, that he could return home to see Dottie and the kids, and that they could begin to be a real family before he had to go on a mission again.

CHAPTER 8

As soon as Jack drew closer to the location of the cabin, he moved slower, listening for any voices or other sounds, indicating any of the perps were about. Wary, he watched for any sign of movement, in case any of them had shifted into cougar form. Though he suspected they wouldn't be running as cougars right now.

Not hearing anything except for the breeze stirring the pine needles, a hawk screeching way above the tall pines, and the flow of the river nearby, he moved in even closer. When he reached sight of the cabin, he stared at the parking area where the vehicles would have been. They were gone. *Hell.*

Still, he had to be sure that they hadn't left anyone behind. He crept closer to the cabin, listening for any sound that might indicate someone was still inside. He heard a light moaning. Now what?

Someone was dying? Or having sex?

Jack listened for any sign of his partners. Nothing. If someone was dying inside, he had to save him...or her. If for nothing more than to learn where the others had gone and what they were up to.

He reached the window on silent padded paws and put them against the window frame, looking in. He couldn't see anyone in the living room. Wait, he thought he saw a boot by the end of the couch. No movement. No more moans.

Jack waited a moment more, listening, smelling the scents—Hellion's, Gigi's, and two more men's scents. And blood.

Jack looked at the top of the window sash. Locked. He had to chance checking on the man inside so he raced around to the cabin door in front. He leapt onto the deck and shifted in front of it. He twisted the knob and slowly opened it. The hinges creaked, warning anyone inside that someone was coming.

He immediately shifted again, having more protection in his cougar coat than if he was unarmed and naked. He ran around the brown tweed sofa and saw the man who was supposed to be Hellion's partner in crime. Bishop, shot in the forehead, blood all over the wood floor. Jack drew close and listened for the man's heartbeat and tried to detect his breath. He was no longer breathing, his heart no longer beating. Bishop was dead.

One of their perps was down. Except now they didn't have any idea what the rest were up to or where they had gone. Jack checked out the two bedrooms and bathroom in the cabin, no sign of bags or anything else, so it looked like the others had left for good. At least Jack and his team had their license tags so they could try and run them down that way.

He heard footfalls, light. He still could detect them as they moved toward the cabin. He peeked out the window and saw Leyton in the shrubs off a ways, Travis coming in from a different direction so if they took fire, they wouldn't both be hit. Catching their attention, he got down and went to the door, and hurried out of the cabin to let them know it was safe.

Leyton was carrying a backpack, so he'd have Jack's clothes. They still needed to do a thorough search of the cabin to ensure nothing had been left behind. Any clue as to where Hellion and the others had gone. Or what they intended to do. He suspected they would be up to no good.

They all joined Jack in the cabin, and Leyton set the backpack down on the couch while Jack shifted, dumped his clothes out, and pulled on his boxer briefs.

"Hell, that's Bishop," Travis said. "Who the hell killed him?" Travis leaned over to make sure he was dead.

"Well, we have the new guy whose identity we don't know, Hellion, and possibly Gigi. I don't know if she can shoot a weapon." Jack pulled on his camo pants. He really liked the "uniform" they wore. Casual, no suits, just their own clothes, and it was up to them. For an assignment like this, his camo clothes were best.

"Did you see anything, hear anything?" Leyton asked, returning from a search of the bedrooms.

"Just this guy moaning. And then I came in to check out the situation. If he was injured, I wanted us to be able to question whoever it was. He'd died by the time I entered the cabin. I'd say they left within the last forty minutes or so. Probably already packed up and ready to go before they decided to get rid of Bishop. Another thing—when Gigi had issues with my mom at the theme park in Branson my last trip there three months ago, we learned she had a boyfriend, Al. She sent him into a restaurant we were eating at to threaten me, but once I straightened him out, he left the park and her behind. So I don't think he's involved." Jack gave them a description of him anyway.

"Okay, good. I'll call Dan and let the sheriff's department take care of Bishop's body." Leyton got on his phone at once.

Jack made another sweep through the place, looking under the beds, unable to keep from smelling the sex Gigi had with the other man in one of the bedrooms. Jack was sure glad he had dumped her when he had. The woman was a real menace and he wondered again how he'd ever thought she was the one for him when he'd asked her to marry him. Maybe it was because she was excited about marrying a military man, and she'd been so enthusiastic about where he was going with the army. So different from Dottie, yet Dottie had been the one who really made him think of nothing else but being with her, and being her mate.

"I think he's gathering wool again," Travis said.

"Hell, you know what it's like to be newly mated," Leyton said, smirking at Jack as he rejoined them in the living room.

"What?" Yeah, Jack had heard them talking. He hadn't heard them ask him any questions.

"Okay, is the guy she was with one of the guys she'd

been seeing while you were engaged to her, before you broke off the engagement because of it?" Travis asked.

Jack glanced back at the bedroom. "Ah, hell."

"Okay, so have you got a name?" Travis asked.

"No. I would know him by scent. I don't know why it didn't dawn on me before." Probably because Jack was smelling Gigi's scent and it was bringing back memories of being with her. But he hadn't known any of the names of the three guys she'd been with. He just knew all three of them by scent. He'd been suspicious when she didn't want to see him at her place, so he'd finally forced the issue. The thing that really annoyed him was she didn't believe she'd done anything wrong. Which, if she'd really felt that way, she wouldn't have hidden the fact she'd had three other men in her bed.

"Dan, Bishop was hit by a single bullet to the head and left to die. He expired right before Jack entered the cabin. Bishop wasn't bitten by a cougar, and there was no evidence of anything left behind. Just him in the cabin. So it's okay to call the county coroner on this one. No one will know he's one of us." Leyton paused on the phone, glanced at Jack, and raised his brows. "Yeah, Jack's still with us, no gunshot wounds or cougar bites or anything. Same with the rest of us, if you're interested." He smiled. "An hour? No lead on where Hellion and the others took off to. But Jack and Trevor both got a license plate number from the two vehicles. Chuck has Chet running them down for us. We'll sit tight for now. See you soon."

Jack checked the man's pockets for anything. He found car and house keys. He held them up and jiggled them.

"Once we have an address, we could check it out. Though no telling where he lives. Dan and Stryker are on their way." Leyton got a call while Jack went outside to search around the parking area just in case anyone dropped anything.

"Okay, thanks, Chet. I'll let the team know. Jack? Well, he's a go-getter."

Jack smiled.

"All right, we have one dead Bishop here. It looks like Hellion's hooked up with this new guy. Ralph Solo? Real name or some kind of joke? Okay, thanks."

"Nothing that I could find out there," Jack said.

"The new guy is Ralph Solo, and he's had some traffic violations, nothing major, no jail time. His place is located in Loveland. So I figure we'll head out there and see if we can find any information on what he was up to."

"Loveland?" Jack was surprised that the guy was living in Colorado when he'd been seeing Gigi in Missouri at the same time Jack was engaged to her. Maybe Ralph moved there, or back here after having some fun with Gigi there. Ralph would have probably known her brother too. Which was another reason they were all working together.

"Yeah, they have a fair amount of cougars there too. He might have been from there originally."

"And taking college courses in Missouri also." Jack pulled out his phone to call Dottie. "Hey, Dottie, all of us are fine here. We located Bishop, the one who was Jeffrey's partner. He's dead, his new partners killed him. I suspect Hellion, or the other guy with him, wanted to be in charge. Just so you know, Hellion's new partner is a man called Ralph Solo. He's one of the men who was Gigi's lover when we were engaged and she was here too."

"Omigod, Jack. I know him."

"Ralph Solo?" Jack couldn't have been more surprised to learn Dottie knew him.

"Yeah, he was taking some of the same core courses as me and so we had a few classes together—English lit, geology, world history. I saw him kissing a girlfriend in the hallway outside our classroom the one time."

"Hell, don't tell me—she was blond-haired, green-eyed, slender build?"

"Sounds like her. He never said her name when I saw them around each other. I guess it was Gigi. When I saw her at the theme park, I didn't realize she was the same woman."

"Can you give a description of what he looked like?"

"Dark-haired, tall, lanky, cougar, like us, narrow face, blue eyes. So Hellion or Ralph killed Bishop?"

"One of them did. Gigi, maybe, though I don't know if she knows how to shoot a gun. So maybe one of the guys did it. We're waiting on Dan and Stryker to get here and then we'll head out."

"Okay, just be careful."

"I will. Are the kids there? Can I talk to them?"

She laughed. "Yes. Bouncing up and down, eager to talk with you."

He smiled, glad they weren't upset with him for not seeing them right away.

Trish said, "Hello?"

"Hey, Trish, I can't wait to see you. Are you helping your mom out?"

"Yeah. We baked cookies. Mommy says if you're not home in time, we get to eat them all up. And we can make more for you."

Jack chuckled. "That's good. I can't wait to eat some."

"Here's Jeff."

"Why aren't you home yet? You said you'd be home." Jeff wasn't happy with him.

"I was. And I moved in. Then I had to catch the bad guys."

"Did you catch them?" Jeff asked, sounding hopeful.

"Not yet. Soon, we hope."

"Okay. Mom says I gotta go."

"Love you and Trish and Mom."

"Hey," Dottie said.

"I'm glad they're not too upset with me for not being there when they came home."

"They said they weren't leaving like that again, so they wouldn't miss you again."

"I love you and the kids, Dottie. I'll be home as soon as I can."

"Be safe," she said again.

When he ended the call, the guys were both smiling at him. "What? I saw you texting Kate earlier. And Travis called his better half twice already."

They laughed. "Yeah, we did, or we'd get hell when we

got home," Leyton said. "I know you have searched around the area. Let's do it again."

"I'm going to shift again and search out a little bit farther." Jack liked to get close to the ground, smell where everyone had walked, see if anyone had moved away from the area and not just been moving closer to the cabin.

By the time Jack had stripped and shifted, the other guys were outside looking for any clues they'd missed. He headed way out to try and locate anything farther away. He found cigarette butts that Bishop had smoked under a group of aspen, his boot prints, and a couple of other size boot prints too. It looked like the men had all come out here and talked for a while. The grass was tamped down, and ten cigarette butts were in the grass. From the smell of them, the only one smoking had been Bishop.

A car engine rumbled, and Jack was glad Dan and Stryker had arrived to take care of the body. He wanted to go to Loveland and search through this guy's place, take care of this business, and head on home to Dottie and the kids. Continuing to look for any other clues in a widening sweep of the area, he heard shots fired back at the cabin. Crap!

He raced back to the cabin, assuming Hellion and the others had returned to dispose of the body, or thought they'd left something behind that would incriminate them.

The silver Ford Taurus tore down the gravel road out of there as Leyton and Travis tried to hit the tires. The car disappeared around a bend in the road beyond the pine trees.

His fellow agents looked okay, so Jack raced through the woods to see which road the perp would take at the junction. Well away from the road in the direction of the junction, he dove through the pine and firs and aspen.

The car reached the fork and turned right. Suddenly, the passenger's window rolled down. Jack didn't expect Gigi to catch sight of him, or to ready a gun and shoot at him. Not because he didn't think she hated him enough to do so, but because he really hadn't believed she could shoot or that she really was into killing people.

As many rounds as she fired at him, clipping the tree trunks, branches, and twigs, he knew she wasn't trying to just injure him. He dove back through the trees, getting far enough away that she couldn't hit him. *Damn the woman.*

He loped back to the cabin, and finally reached it and saw Leyton on his cell, calling in the situation to Dan. Travis must have been inside the cabin. Jack ran into the house to shift and dress so he could tell Leyton which direction the driver had driven. Inside, Travis was sitting on the couch looking a bit dazed, a bloodied bandage secured to the side of his forehead.

Hell. Jack hadn't thought either of them had been wounded or he would have stayed to help out. Travis must have had his head turned so that Jack hadn't seen where he'd been hit.

Jack shifted, then threw on his boxer briefs and called out to Leyton. "He took the right fork at the road." Then he hurried over to Travis, took hold of his wrist, and checked his pulse. "How bad are you hurt?"

Travis grunted. "I swear I have to get one of these every mission just to remind myself I'm still alive and working a dangerous job. It's just a graze but head wounds bleed a lot. And I was getting a little dizzy. Which is the only reason I'm sitting on the couch."

"Nothing for you to do right now anyway."

Leyton came into the cabin and nodded to Jack. "Thanks for getting the direction they were heading in."

"I might not have gone after them if I'd known Travis had been shot. Hell, Gigi was shooting at me too, so she might have even been the one who killed Bishop. I found cigarette butts by some trees out back. All were Bishop's. But

I didn't find anything else."

"We weren't expecting them to return. Naturally. They saw Travis near the parking area and of course, they had no idea who he was. They probably assumed he was just a hiker. If Bishop had been alive, he would have recognized both Travis and me. Anyway, they began shooting at Travis, and he went down. They started to get out of the car to finish him off, when I came around the other side of the cabin and began shooting at them. They dove back into the vehicle and took off down the road."

"Tell me you hit someone." Jack finished getting dressed.

"I did. But, like with us, they're cougars. Faster healing abilities. Though I hit Ralph in the left arm, so it'll take a little longer for him to heal up."

"My head's killing me. I'll be fine after a few hours," Travis said.

"You'll go back with Dan and see Kate." Leyton was in charge and though Travis didn't appear to like the idea as sour as he looked, he just slumped back against the couch in a defeated posture.

"I have Jack to watch my back, so you don't have to worry about me," Leyton said.

Jack suspected that it was more than that. Travis wanted to be one of the ones to take the men down. He didn't blame him. Jack felt the same way.

Twenty minutes later, Dan and Stryker drove up, then entered the cabin. Dan said, "The coroner is on the way. Hell, Travis, you look like you took a beating. Don't let Bridget see you or she'll know she should have been out here with you watching your back."

"If you have everything under control here, we're heading to Bishop's house in Loveland. We'll let you know what we find." Leyton looked at Travis. "Are you going to be all right?"

"Yeah, you know me. I'll be raring to go in a few hours. Don't do all the work before I'm back on the job."

Leyton smiled at him, then he and Jack headed back to where they'd left the car.

"I sure hoped you'd taken them out. So what happened to Hellion?" Jack climbed into the passenger's seat.

Leyton got into the driver's seat and they took off for Loveland. "He didn't return. I suspect Ralph and Gigi came back for the body. I don't know why they would have returned otherwise."

"For something they'd left behind? Though we couldn't

find anything. You don't want to try following them first, do you?"

"No. They have too much of a head start. We go to Loveland like we had planned."

"Why didn't they take care of the body the first time around? Why come back for it?" Jack couldn't imagine they got spooked, left, and then returned unless they'd needed something to wrap the body in and didn't want to use anything from the rental cabin. Might be too suspicious.

"Maybe they had second thoughts about leaving a body behind. Or maybe they hadn't planned to kill him and didn't have anything to wrap the body in. They decided they didn't want to get blood in the trunk of the car. You know, it could be that he fought with them about who was in charge or what they were going to do. Then the disagreement was resolved permanently."

Jack pulled out his phone and looked up the nearest hardware store. He called the store and said, "I'm Jack Barrington with a special police force investigating a local crime. Can you tell me if anyone recently purchased a tarp, maybe a roll of tape also?"

"For a dead body? Oh, I know I let my imagination go wild sometimes. When the man and woman checked out, that's the first thing I thought of. They were here about a half hour ago. Maybe a little longer."

"We'll be right there." Jack ended the call and Leyton glanced at him, probably wondering when he'd agreed to go to the hardware store. "The store is located in the direction Ralph went. It won't take us but another half hour to go there."

Leyton shook his head. "Somehow, I had the impression you were working for me. And this is your first training mission."

"I am. So it's your call."

Leyton headed for the hardware store at the junction of the roads. "I take it that Ralph bought a tarp and tape at the store."

"Yep. And the clerk even assumed the man and woman were going to take care of a dead body."

Leyton smiled.

"Vivid imagination. But if it was them, he was right on the money."

When they arrived at the store, Leyton showed the clerk a picture of Hellion, Bishop, and Ralph, courtesy of Chet who sent them a picture of his driver's license photo on file.

"Okay, yeah, that guy was the one who bought the tarp

and tape."

"But not the other man?" Jack asked. "What about the woman?" He pulled up an old Facebook photo of her.

"Yeah, that's her. The other two guys were in here a few days ago. They were getting just the usual stuff. A couple of grocery items."

"If you see any of these people in here again, call us." Leyton handed him a card. "They're armed and extremely dangerous. So no heroics. Just wait until they've left the store."

"Yes, sir."

"We don't believe they'll return, but just in case. Did they say anything that you can recall?" Jack asked right before they left.

"The man and woman who came in today were arguing with each other. Oh, God, they really did kill someone. That's what the tarp was for."

"What did they say?" Leyton hurried to ask.

"The guy said if her brother was going to keep going off the deep end... Then she told him not to worry. It had always been the plan. I was stacking some floor heaters on the shelves, and the man and woman were on the other side of the shelves in the next aisle over. Then we got busy and I got called up to the front to help check out people. They ended up in my line. He said to her that he wasn't always going to clean up his messes. She just looked stormy-faced and didn't answer him. Then he said, 'Do you understand?' And she said, 'I heard you the first time, all right?' I just figured it was a couple having an argument. My brother and his girlfriend have them all the time.

"Then they paid cash and the two of them stalked out of here. A few minutes later, she returned to buy a candy bar and a soda. Then she left."

"Thank you for all your help," Leyton said. "Just call us if you see any of them. Don't, whatever you do, try to make a citizen's arrest."

When they left the store, Leyton said, "Good call about getting some more intel from the hardware store. At least now we know your ex-fiancée didn't kill Bishop. Her brother did."

"No. She just tried to kill me."

"I bet she was thrilled to see you." Leyton smiled as they got on the road again.

"I think that's why it took her so long to shoot at me. She was so shocked to see me in the woods there too that it took her a moment to react. Once she did, she was shooting up everything behind me. Thankfully, I made it out of her range quickly enough. They're probably trying to figure out who you are and then now what I'm doing here with the two of you guys when the last she knew, I was in the army."

"Well, if they hadn't killed Bishop, he would have known about Travis and me, at least." They drove in silence for some time, then Leyton spoke up again. "You know that Dottie gave up her degree plans because of you. Basically because she learned she was pregnant and she was afraid that Hellion might learn of it."

"Yeah, we haven't discussed it. If she wants to go back to college, she can."

"What about work?"

"That's up to her. I already told her I'd support her so she could stay home with the kids. And when I'm not on a mission, I'll stay with them. She's free to have some fun with the ladies. Whatever she wants to do. I suspect with the baby on the way, and the kids at home, she's going to want to quit."

"Well, Dan and everyone will miss her at the job, but I'm glad she has choices."

"What about you and Kate? Any plans for kids?"

"Eventually. I don't think she'll want to give up her

practice though. She's the only doctor in town, and she wouldn't want to leave everyone in a lurch. Plus, she loves what she does. So for now, we're good."

A call came through for Leyton on his dashboard, and it was Kate. "Hey, honey, after being shot, Travis looks pretty gray, but hopefully, he'll be okay when you run the scan on him," Leyton said.

"Dan said they'd be here soon, Bridget's on her way over, and Travis is talking away like nothing's happened. I'll let you know how he's doing as soon as I examine him. But I had a moment between patients and was calling to tell you something that can't wait. We're having a baby."

Jack laughed out loud.

CHAPTER 9

At the sheriff's department, Dottie had another call from the cat lady, Mrs. Sorenson, third time in two weeks. Dottie knew she wanted to see more of Stryker, since her own son, Mick, Hal and Tracey's boss, who was in charge of taking down animal traffickers, didn't make it into town that often. "I'll have someone check into it right away."

"Send Deputy Hill. He knows how to get to my house."

"I'll see what I can do. He's out on another call right now."

"Not another missing cat case, is it?"

Dottie swore Mrs. Sorenson was afraid some other cat owner meant he'd only have time for another owner's missing cats now. "No."

"Oh, my, all right. Then I can wait for him for a little while

188

longer."

"Good. I'll tell him as soon as we get off the line."

Dottie swore she was going to tell Stryker to ask Mrs. Sorenson out on a date, just to encourage her to quit calling about one of her cats being in the tree or missing in the woods. They eventually got down on their own or came home if none of the deputies could make it in a timely fashion, especially when Mrs. Sorenson put out a bowl of cat food. So everyone knew she was just lonely.

Later that day, Mrs. Sorenson called again about a cat. This time she sounded really excited.

"The one in the tree isn't your cat?" At least that was what Dottie was guessing, since Mrs. Sorenson sounded more excited than usual.

Then Dottie got a call from Dan and she said to Mrs. Sorenson, "Hold on a second, Dan's calling and it might be something crucial to a murder investigation."

"Okay, the cat's not going anywhere."

"Dan, yes?"

"Anything going on?" he asked.

Though Dan knew if there was anything really important going on, Dottie would have told him already. "Just Stryker has another by-request mission—treed cat—"

"Don't tell me. Mrs. Sorenson."

"Yep."

Dan laughed. Then he told her what had happened with the dead body and Travis.

"Travis is okay, from what I hear from Kate. Just got some downtime for a day or two," Dottie said.

"Yeah, he's good. Just needs his mate's loving. Listen, as long as we don't have any dead bodies show up or, Leyton and Jack don't need some help with their case, I need to take care of some personal business so I will need to take off."

"Uh, yeah, sure, Dan. I'll just call one of the part-time deputy sheriffs, if it's nothing too major."

"Good. I'll be back at the office in a couple of days. Just call if it's anything critical."

Dottie was dying to know what was up. Dan never took time off for personal business. He never took any time off ever. She couldn't help being curious about it. That was part of the hazard of being a big cat. Dottie wondered if Stryker knew what was going on. After they ended the call, she got back on the line with Mrs. Sorenson.

"Okay, so not one of your cats?"

"No. I'll send you a picture of it. I looked it up on the Internet. It's a caracal—wild cat. They have them in Africa,

Asia, and India. Some other places. But not in Yuma Town. It's just watching me."

Dottie was looking at the picture of the cat on her computer, not believing the pointy-eared, medium-sized wild cat was in their town. It was beautiful, with tufts of black hair on its long-tapering ears. It looked a little bit like a lynx, but with a long tail, longer legs, and a slenderer body. First the bear, someone reported otters at the lake, an alligator—that was removed—and now this?

"Okay, I'll get Stryker right on it."

"I wonder if someone tried to make it a pet. It's tame enough acting."

"It says here they run like a cheetah. They aren't sprinters like the cheetahs are. If dogs chase them, they climb into the trees. They can leap ten feet. And it says people trained them to hunt birds, antelope, rabbits, and foxes, like they did with the cheetah. So it's possible someone owns it. It's usually nocturnal, which makes me wonder why it's out at this time of day, and in your tree. Anyway, just stay safe. I'll get Stryker to run right over there."

Dottie called Stryker next. "Hey, got a new one from Mrs. Sorenson. It's not about one of her cats this time. A caracal is in her tree."

"A what?"

"Here, I'll send you the photo she sent. Watch out for the claws. It can be between thirteen to forty-four pounds, the males are bigger than the females. So this must be a male, judging by the size."

"What in the world is it doing here?"

"Someone's pet? Has to be a human. I doubt our cougars would own a wild cat for a pet. But it says they've been trained for hunting in other countries, much like the cheetahs. So it's possible someone has it as a pet and it got away from him."

"As a hunting cat? I'm almost there. Can you call me if there's a cute, single cougar that needs rescuing next time?"

Dottie smiled. "Yeah, sure, I'll put that on my list of calls you need to take care of. I'd be careful of tranquilizing him unless you're really sure about his weight though." Not that she needed to tell Stryker his job. Tranquilizing any animal could be deadly if they didn't use the right dose.

Ten minutes later, Stryker called her back. "I'm just pulling up now."

A car door slammed shut. She heard Stryker's footfalls, and then he stopped. "Beautiful golden eyes. Brick-red coat, white underside and, hell, it's a female. And she's jumping!"

A shot was fired off.

Dottie prayed that the cat would be okay. Well, and that Stryker was too.

"Got her. Aww, hell. About four-foot ten, redhead, golden eyes, naked woman."

Dottie's jaw dropped. "Omigod. Okay, calling it in to Dan." This was amazing. She knew he'd want to hear about it. Before she could call him, she had another incoming call.

It was Mrs. Fitzgerald, who was the resident Yuma Town gossip.

"Oh, Dottie, did Dan tell you about the blond staying with him? She came in late last night. She walked right into his house like she lived there. He wasn't even home at the time. Surprised me to pieces. Do you think he's seeing someone now that you're married to Jack? But listen to me. I completely forgot why I called. I'm arranging a baby shower for you and I just wondered if we should invite Dan's friend." Mrs. Fitzgerald was a platinum blond, vivacious woman who just turned sixty-seven. She was always smiling, widowed, and ran the coffee and pastry shop in town, Fitz's Pastry and Coffee Shop. She prided herself on her to-die-for pastries.

Dottie often picked up pastries for everyone at the sheriff's department. They all ran off the calories as cougars, so no problem there. The coffee shop was a fun gathering place for afternoon or evening dessert and was always crowded with both out-of-town guests and locals. Even while supervising the baking operation, or mixing up a great latte, Mrs. Fitzgerald always had time to visit with everyone for a few minutes.

But about Dan? Dottie couldn't have been more surprised. "She might just be someone who is visiting for a brief time and then will be gone. I wouldn't worry about it." Dottie now suspected that was the reason for him needing some personal time.

"Well, I wouldn't want to exclude her, if it turns out she's going to be staying around for any length of time. You know how tight-knit we are and we don't want to leave anyone out and hurt their feelings."

Dottie sighed. Mrs. Fitzgerald was definitely one of the most agreeable people like that. Even if the cougar didn't fit in really well, she wanted to make him or her welcome.

"I mean, I figured you could ask Dan on account of you work for him and get along so well."

"Which means he'll tell me if she's staying around for a while and we need to include her. Otherwise, don't plan on it." At least Dottie didn't think the woman was going to stay if Dan said he only needed to take a couple of days off to deal with personal business. So was this the reason? Dottie was dying to know who she was, but she wouldn't ask Dan. "Got to go."

"All right. You take care, dear."

"You, too." Dottie was dying to ask Shannon if she knew anything because Chase was a part-time deputy sheriff and Dan might have told him and Chase might have told his mate. Still, Dottie wasn't going to start spreading stories about Dan. Not that she wouldn't talk to Jack about it when he got home. He wouldn't know what Dan was doing anyway. It was just something she would talk to her mate about. She suspected Jack still wondered if there had been any dating between her and Dan. So maybe if Dan was seeing someone now, that would put any concern Jack might have to rest, if he was worried about Dan in the least.

She called Dan up to let him know about the caracal, wishing he'd tell her about the blond at his home. "Dan, Stryker just tranquilized a caracal."

"A what?"

"One of those cats from Africa with the pointy ears like a lynx, but it's bigger. She turned into a naked woman."

"Okay, as long as Stryker's got a handle on it."

TERRY SPEAR

Dottie couldn't believe it! Either the blond was just too hot to take his eyes and hands off, or something else was going on. She really couldn't understand his indifference. "Okay." She decided right then and there she wasn't calling the sheriff about anything else unless someone was killed or they had a major evacuation of Yuma Town or something else that was catastrophic.

Stryker called her back. "I'm taking her to see the doc. Kate can decide what to do next."

"Hey, you said you wanted me to send you to a job with a—"

"Cougar shifter. Not a caracal shifter."

"Picky, picky." She laughed. "Okay. If I don't manage to call Kate before you do, let me know how the woman is doing, and what she's doing here."

"What did Dan say?"

"You know he's off on personal business, right?" Dottie assumed Dan had already told Stryker he had to be off for a couple of days.

"Uh, yeah. But I figured this was pretty interesting, if nothing else."

"Well, you heard about the blond at his home, didn't you?"

196

"Blond? Hell, no. Don't tell me. He didn't care anything about the caracal? Did you interrupt anything then?" Stryker laughed. "And Dan gives *me* a hard time!"

"I just figured you would know about it. Mrs. Fitzgerald was the one who told me and she spread the word, I figured. But maybe she hasn't."

"Huh, well, I won't say anything to anyone. That's definitely interesting news. I'd say if he wants to keep this private, we need to let it go. He'll tell us if he feels we need to know."

"Okay, I agree. So is the caracal shifter woman older, younger? Pretty?"

Stryker laughed. "She's beautiful. And a wild cat. She reminds me a little of Shannon. But younger. Maybe an older teen."

"Oh, not another cougar on the run then? Except she's a different kind of wild cat?"

"I wouldn't think she'd be sitting in a tree at a home on the outskirts of town. Why not hunkered down in the rocks or caves out by the lake? In the woods, sleeping in a tree?"

"Why would she be here at all?" Dottie asked.

"Good question. I'll drop by and check on her in a couple of hours when she's more alert."

"Why did you shoot her?"

Stryker didn't say right away.

Dottie laughed. "Okay, give it to me straight or I'll ask Mrs. Sorenson what happened. And we'll learn soon enough from the cat herself."

"She jumped me. Or...tried. She leapt straight at me before I even had a chance to clear the car. I swung the rifle up and shot her with one dart. She dropped on top of the rack on the car. Truthfully, I wasn't sure how I was going to deal with the cat in the tree. It's not like rescuing a housecat. But then the caracal decided it for me."

"Just think, from this beginning there could be little caracal-cougar shifter babies."

"Not likely."

Dottie figured Stryker was still wondering about the woman who had come through here when he was playing Santa Claus for grownup ladies for charity. When he was asked if he wanted to do the charity Santa bit this year, he was all for it. What would the chances be that the woman would show up again and drop by the place where he was showing off his well-toned Santa muscles?

"Hey, Hal's here at the clinic with Tracey. She's having more contractions. I'm going to drop by and see them, and then I'll just be patrolling the area, and you can let me know if anything needs my attention."

"What did you do about the bear?"

"He was gone by the time I reached the location where he'd been seen. Someone said he'd taken off into the woods. He hasn't attacked anyone—yet, not bothered anyone's dogs, so I'm not chasing him down."

"Hey, just got another call. Traffic accident in front of the coffee shop. Lots of eyewitnesses."

"Off to check it out."

Then Dottie got a call from Jack. "Hey, honey, we haven't reached Loveland yet. We're checking out the dead man's house there. Since I didn't have any news, I figured there was no sense in bothering you," Jack said.

"You are never bothering me. Hey, have you ever heard of a caracal shifter?"

"No. Don't tell me they exist."

"Stryker just tranquilized one in a tree. Which was kind of how Chase met Shannon. Except she was up in some cliffs when Chase shot her. Luckily, no humans were around at the time when this woman shifted. She's at the clinic now."

"Sounds like it's a lot more interesting than here. Hold on," Jack said. "Leyton wants the story." Jack explained to

TERRY SPEAR

Leyton, "Apparently Stryker tranquilized a caracal, and she shifted into her human form."

Leyton laughed in the background.

"She's all right though, isn't she?" Jack asked.

"Yeah," Dottie said. "She's fine. We just don't have a clue why she's here or who she is."

"Everyone in Yuma Town will want to see her in her cat form. Except for seeing a caracal in a zoo one time, that's the only instance where I've ever observed the wild cat," Jack said.

"Me too," Leyton agreed. "I'm calling Kate now for an update. I still can't believe Kate's having a baby."

Dottie said, "What?"

"She just told me."

"Omigod, Leyton, I'm so happy for you. You will make a great papa."

"I still can't believe it."

Jack laughed. "Welcome to fatherhood."

There was no such thing as patient confidentiality among the shifters. Well, for some things, sure. Concerning the health of an unknown shifter, to ensure a shifter who needed further care was taken care of by other shifters when they were discharged? That was shared with the people who needed to know.

"Okay, if you learn anything about the caracal, let me know."

Twenty minutes later, she got a call from Stryker saying he'd taken care of the traffic accident, and he was going on patrol and that someone had spotted the bear again.

She hoped they didn't have to take him down.

Jack called to give her a heads up that they had just reached Bishop's house and he'd update her after they left there. Dottie prayed he and Leyton didn't run into real trouble there.

CHAPTER 10

When Dottie got Bridget's return call, she suspected it was about Travis and his head injury again. "Hey, Bridget, is he all right?"

Bridget snorted. "I can't believe he was going to try and hide it from me. Thanks for calling me right away to tell me he'd been injured. But yes, Kate said he was all right. I just need to keep him on bedrest for overnight. He told me that Jack is a bit of a maverick, but that at least he doesn't get shot."

Dottie breathed a sigh of relief. She had no idea how Jack would react on the job. As the Yuma Town police dispatcher, she'd been surprised when she got the call from Leyton asking for Dan's assistance in the case of a dead

Bishop. She figured that Hellion, or the other guy, Ralph, had a falling out with Bishop and took him down. Until Dan had called back with news that Hellion had killed Bishop, per an update from Leyton.

She wondered how long it would take Leyton and Jack to bring down the two men, and from what Dan had said, Jack's ex-fiancée too. Dottie couldn't believe the woman had been shooting at Jack also. After five years, Gigi was still angry with them? She had to be as unbalanced as her brother.

On the other hand, Dottie wished that Travis was with Leyton and Jack still. If they were just checking out Bishop's house, she thought that wouldn't be too dangerous. As long as Hellion and others didn't show up there.

"How are you doing?" Bridget asked.

"Don't tell Jack. I'm growing so big, so fast, I'm certain I'm having twins again."

Bridget laughed. "I won't tell. But you're not going to wait until they're born, are you?"

"No. Just until I have an ultrasound that proves I'm having twins. No sense in unduly worrying him."

Bridget laughed again. "I hope he won't be too shocked. I'm sure Travis would be if I told him the news."

"What news?" Travis asked in the background.

"Nothing, Travis. Just girl talk. I have to go since Travis is awake, and make sure he doesn't need anything."

"All right. Give him a hug for me." Dottie hoped Jack was all right with having twins, if she was having them. They didn't have any choice anyway. She wished her aunt lived nearby if she ended up with two sets of twins. Especially if Jack was away a lot on missions.

***

"This is the address," Jack said, pointing to the red brick, one-story house when they arrived at Bishop's home.

The blinds and curtains were all drawn in the three windows that faced the street. The grass needed to be mowed, but so did half the neighbors' yards. The trees and shrubs were all overgrown for the small lot sizes. Cars and pickups were parked in driveways and street-side for most of the houses, except for Bishop's. At least no one appeared to be home and Hellion and his buddies hadn't come here. Though Ralph and Gigi had headed in the opposite direction so they would have had to drive out of their way to come here.

"Are you ready?" Leyton asked.

"Yeah."

Jack and Leyton got out of the vehicle, shut the doors, and walked up to the front door.

Leyton took Bishop's keys and tried two of the ones that looked like house keys before the second one gained them access. Jack kept thinking they'd have to announce themselves, even if the owner was dead. From what Leyton had told him, they didn't exactly go by police procedures, because they didn't arrest these guys if they were attempted murderers or murderers.

After they moved through the house, first checking all the rooms to make sure they were clear, they finally rejoined each other in the living room.

"No sign that Hellion, his sister, or Ralph have been here," Jack said.

"No. Looks like they met elsewhere. Let's start searching drawers and the like."

"I'll take the bedrooms," Jack said.

"I'll get the kitchen." Leyton stalked into the kitchen while Jack checked out the first bedroom. This one looked like a typical bedroom: bed, night stand, dresser.

In the closet, he found boxes stacked high. He pulled out one and set it on the bed. He tore off the tape sealing the box, opened it up, and saw all kinds of explosive devices. *Hell*.

"Hey, Leyton, you might want to see this."

"What did you find?" Leyton stalked down the hallway toward the bedroom.

"Armaments. And if the rest of the boxes are filled with the same, enough for a small army."

Leyton joined him in the bedroom and took a look at the contents of the box, then he glanced at the other boxes in the closet. "Let's check them all out. This is probably some of the same ordinance that he and Jeffrey used to cause the cave-in at the gold mine where Travis and I had to call for help."

"Was Bishop in the service?"

"Yeah, demolition expert. They were hiding illegal weapons in the mine. When we came to, the men and weapons were gone."

Jack closed up the box and retrieved another from the closet while Leyton opened one too. "It might have taken a while. It appears we've confiscated it for good this time. As long as we can get a team to secure it before we have any trouble," Leyton said.

Jack looked at all the semi-automatics and was glad they'd found this before these bastards could sell them to criminals who would use them on innocents next.

***

When Dottie got home from work, she thanked Abby Rodgers and checked to see what all the kids had learned today. Abby was teaching them their letters, numbers, and coins. And she'd been working with them on printing letters and learning to tell time.

Jeff pointed at the oven clock. "It's four-fifteen."

"Very good."

Trish said. "It's four-sixteen."

Dottie smiled. "Yes, it's a minute later." It was amazing how much she took for granted and she remembered Aunt Emily always saying she was born knowing these things.

"What are we having for supper?" Jeff asked.

"Spaghetti." She gave them apple halves and a cheese stick to tide them over. They were always hungry, it seemed.

"Yum." Trish sat at the table to eat her snack.

"Can we have pizza tomorrow?" Jeff asked.

"Yes. I'll have to pick one up."

"Is Daddy coming home to eat with us?" Trish asked.

"I don't think so. But you never know." Dottie could only hope. She hadn't ever felt that needy before and though she kept telling herself she should stop feeling that way, just get done whatever needed to be done, she couldn't help wanting him home.

***

"Okay, we have to call this armament cache in. I'll let Chuck know we need some men to take care of this arsenal. In case there's anything else, keep looking through the boxes for any clues as to what they planned to do with this stuff. I'm going to check the other rooms some more," Leyton said to Jack.

"All right. Will do." Jack couldn't believe the veritable minefield they had here.

Leyton headed out of the room.

Jack found ammo, grenades, and all sorts of different guns, when he heard someone running down the hall. He immediately pulled out his Glock.

"Me," Leyton said, his voice low. "Men are sneaking in the back way."

"They have to know our car is out front," Jack said, loading up a semi-automatic with rounds. He was going to be well-prepared to take out Hellion and Ralph if it was them.

"They came in the back alley. They might not figure anyone's here."

"We can't let them take all of this with them," Jack said.

Leyton nodded. "Our men will be arriving in an hour. I

alerted them we have trouble. Chuck called in the local police. He said it's too volatile a situation for us to handle on our own."

"Which room?" a man in the hallway asked, someone they didn't recognize. That meant they'd picked up another man for the job.

"I have no idea. Just start with the first one and work your way back. Might be some stuff in the attic." It was Hellion's voice.

"I'll check the attic," Ralph said.

A dark-haired and bearded man walked into the bedroom, and Leyton motioned for him to drop his weapon, but the guy tried to shoot him. Leyton shot him in the arm. He cried out and sank to his knees, screaming in pain, dropping his gun. Jack moved to get his gun.

"What the hell's going on?" Hellion called out. He didn't make a move to go to the bedroom, but suddenly sprayed rounds at the wall from the hallway. Both Leyton and Jack ducked into the empty closet.

One of the bullets ricocheted off the door jamb and hit the injured man. He collapsed face down on the carpet and didn't move.

Sirens wailed. Someone fired again at the outer

bedroom wall, then boots ran down the hallway. "Clear out," Hellion shouted.

"But the weapons."

"Cops are coming. Clear out."

Jack raced into the hall and fired at Ralph, catching him in the shoulder.

"Shit." Ralph whipped around to fire at Jack, but Jack shot him in the arm. Ralph dropped his gun and ran out after Hellion.

Leyton and Jack raced down the hall. The men were already in a blue SUV by the time Jack and Leyton ran outside. Jack thought the driver was Gigi as they took off.

Police swarmed around the house and Leyton identified himself and Jack, both of them showing off their badges.

After that, Jack checked the pulse on the wounded man in the bedroom. He was dead. "Did you find anything that can tell us what they were going to do with this stuff?" Jack asked Leyton as the police cordoned off the area and Chuck's special federal task force arrived and took over. They had documents that looked like they belonged to a real government agency.

"If it's anything that Jeffrey was involved in, these guys are all selling weapons illegally. From the looks of it, this has been sitting here for a while though. The tape and boxes are older. No recent smells in the house indicating that Bishop had been here. Like while he went to jail?"

"Why didn't anyone find all of this before, when Bishop was under investigation?" Jack asked.

"His driver's license was just issued so it gave this address." Leyton flipped through his phone. "But for his court records, he had another address listed."

"Okay, so there has to be someone on the outside who has been paying his property taxes, the mortgage, and utility bills, yard maintenance, just to keep up appearances."

"Maybe one of the other guys who was here. Then again, I didn't smell their scents when we first arrived." Leyton looked through the dead man's clothes and found ID. "John Smith. He's from Denver. Hellion was in jail, so he wouldn't have been here taking care of it."

"If he had a partner in crime taking care of it, why not just sell it out from under him? You think whoever it was feared him getting out and retaliating?" Jack asked.

"Or, someone who was extremely loyal to him."

"A brother, father maybe?" Jack wouldn't be surprised.

"Or a mother or sister. I smell the scent of a woman, though it's probably closer to a couple of months since she was here last."

"Could be. Some correspondence is located in a desk drawer in an office." Leyton led him to the office while Chuck's team confiscated all the weapons and loaded them up in a van.

Leyton opened a desk drawer and pulled out some greeting cards and letters and dumped them on top of the desk.

"Letters to him while he was in prison from one Anine Parker. Girlfriend? And some from his mother, all signed Mom." Jack looked through the envelopes. "Anine is in Alaska. Looks like she's one of those women who hook up with guys in jail. In one case I know of, the woman was in prison because her husband raped and murdered several teen girls. She witnessed it, never tried to report it, and she even helped him. So what does she do? She hooks up with a guy in prison, corresponding with him after he'd murdered his girlfriend, while her own husband is in for life. Unfortunately, she's as sick as he is and only got twelve years." Jack looked up the address for the mother. "It looks like Bishop's momma lives three streets over from here." Jack showed the location on his cell's GPS. "But if Bishop hadn't returned home yet, how would the letters have gotten here?"

"Mailed to his mom maybe? And she just dumped them in his desk drawer. A woman's scent is all over them."

"I'd say that was a fair bet. Now whether she knew he had all the weapons stashed in here, that's another story. If he's in prison and she has to take care of the property while he's locked up, don't you think she'd be curious about what was in the house?" Jack would certainly have been.

"Yeah. Let's go see her." After Leyton talked to Chuck's men and the police officers, they drove the short distance to Bishop's mother's place and parked. When they reached the front door, Leyton rang the doorbell.

In a housecoat and slippers, a woman answered, her gray hair mussed up, her gray eyes narrowed as she stared at them. "What do you want?"

Leyton showed his official ID. "We know your son was dealing in stolen weapons."

She tried to close the door in his face. He pushed his way in, Jack following, and he shut and locked the door.

Jack was half expecting to see Hellion again. Maybe Hellion didn't know Bishop's mother lived close by and was taking care of her son's place while he had been incarcerated—if she had been.

"I'm not saying anything that will incriminate my son. He's not done anything wrong. He did his time. Leave him alone."

"Are you aware his house is filled with weapons that we've just confiscated?" Leyton asked.

She glowered at him.

"You don't need to protect your son any longer. One of the men he hooked up with from jail killed him," Jack said.

The woman collapsed on the leather sofa and looked shell-shocked.

"Because of what he was involved in and the kind of people he was dealing with, you have to know he was living on borrowed time." Leyton crouched in front of her as if he wasn't in charge and just wanted to help her out.

"You're cops. You wanted him dead."

"Worse. We're with the CSF."

Her eyes widened.

The CSF was known to remove the criminal cougar element permanently from society, not just give them the luxury of going to jail. It was just too dangerous for the rest of them if the murderous criminals were incarcerated and shifted so they could take care of any menace easily if someone was bothering them in prison.

"Now, you can tell us what you know about the whole operation, or we can take you into custody. You know we have the right to keep our kind safe."

"I don't know anything about it."

"Fine." Leyton brought out a plastic tie.

"You can't arrest me. I told you, I don't know anything about it."

"That's fine. Our interrogation staff will take over and question you further. That's not our job. They have techniques to make people spill their guts that I don't even want to get into."

"Besides," Jack said, wondering if they really did have an interrogation staff, "once Hellion learns you know all about the operation"—he held his hand up to stop her from objecting—"he'll come back for you. He killed your son, and he won't hesitate to kill you."

"All I know is what Bishop did before he went to prison. I went to his trial."

"What about Anine Parker?" Leyton handed her a letter to Bishop from the woman.

Mrs. Adkins read the note and gave it back to Leyton. "He never met her. She's one of those groupies who fantasize about having sex with an inmate."

215

"You didn't know what was stashed in your son's house? You've been paying the taxes and mortgage on the place. Correct?" Jack asked. "Someone had to."

"Sure. It didn't mean I went inside. I didn't even have a key."

"Your scent was in the house," Jack said.

Caught up in the lie, she ground her teeth. "I had to make sure the pipes didn't freeze in the winter. I went into the kitchen and the bathroom. That was it."

"Okay, so what do you know about Hellion Crichton or Ralph Solo?" Leyton asked.

"Nothing. When it came to the kind of work my son was doing, he didn't involve me. Why would he? He wouldn't have wanted me to go to prison."

"How do you pay for his mortgage and taxes?" Jack asked.

She pursed her lips.

Jack and Leyton waited. But not for long. "So you were getting money and then laundering it from your son's arms deals." Leyton helped her to stand and tied her hands in front of her. Then he got on his phone. "We need you to have someone from the special interrogation unit pick up Mrs. Adkins for further questioning. She is involved up to her

216

eyebrows in laundering the money for her son." He gave them the address.

Jack helped Mrs. Adkins sit back down.

"All right. That Hellion you were talking about, I told my son he was a bad one. He just looked mean. Like a bully. Bishop was always good to me. No matter what else he did, he was always kind to me. But Hellion, he scorned me. He had an obvious dislike for the closeness my son and I shared."

"You met him?" Jack asked, shocked. "You're lucky he didn't come here next and shoot you."

"He...he didn't know I lived here. I met them at the cabin a couple of weeks ago. That sister of his, Gigi too. She's a viper. Quiet, but she listens to everything. Narrowed cat eyes. I didn't trust her."

"Ralph Solo is her boyfriend and part of this. Do you know him?" Leyton asked.

"He was there too. Yeah. Bishop didn't tell Hellion where he had the weapons stashed. He didn't entirely trust him. Bishop's old partner, Butch, had been in charge. But this time, my son was. Then Hellion comes along, and I can tell he wants to be running the show. I told Bishop that Hellion did. He just waved it off and said he wouldn't have any trouble with him. Hellion had nothing to bring to the table. No weapons. No contacts. No nothing. Does that matter? No. All Hellion sees is money. I warned my son about him. I hope you kill that SOB." Then Mrs. Adkins broke into tears.

Jack suspected Mrs. Adkins really had loved her son. Too bad he hadn't been a decent sort, and not into criminal activities. And she was just as guilty.

"Do you know where we might find them?" Jack asked.

"That cabin out west of here."

"That's where Hellion killed Bishop," Leyton said.

She shook her head. "That's all he talked about—going there to finalize some plans."

"Can you tell us anything about Butch and why he returned for his wife Dottie and the kids in Yuma Town?" Jack asked.

"She was helping him by being his cover story. He knew those kids weren't his. So he agreed to lie about it and be her husband. Just on paper. But he was killed going back for her and the kids. They were eager to see Butch. Bishop told him not to. That it would be too dangerous. And look what happened to him!"

Two of Chuck's men arrived at the house, and the one said, "We're the agents from the special interrogation unit." He looked tough and all business. Jack swore he was fighting a smile.

When Jack and Leyton left the men to handle Mrs. Adkins, Leyton said to Jack, "I wouldn't believe Mrs. Adkins concerning Dottie. Mrs. Adkins received the information from her rotten son. Maybe that's what Butch told Bishop. Who knows. In any event, Dottie thought he was returning to her originally. She never knew he was a criminal. When he didn't return, she divorced him and never looked back."

"I don't believe Mrs. Adkins either. She either was confused, Bishop told her wrong, or Butch did. In any event, Dottie wouldn't have been eager to see him. So what happens to the money?"

"That's how we get our funding. We sell off the properties, confiscate the cash, use it to fund the CSF."

"Makes sense. Where are we going to now?"

"Home. Until we can come up with another plan."

"At least we confiscated their stash of armaments and took down another one of those men, and have Bishop's mother in custody. Maybe they'll learn something further from her. Jog her memory a bit."

"We don't use torture," Leyton assured him.

Jack smiled. "I didn't really think so, but it's good to hear."

***

When they arrived that night, it was midnight and Jack called to let Dottie know he was coming in so as not to scare her. He was glad to learn how much he'd cheered her with the news.

As soon as he drove up in the driveway, she rushed out to see him in her robe and slippers, her long hair curling about her shoulders, and she looked totally loveable. He scooped her up and carried her in the house, kissing her all the way.

"Are the kids sound asleep?"

"Yes."

"I want to see them." Jack had wanted to see them after they'd gotten married and before he had to go on the mission. He didn't want to chance getting a call to go out again and miss seeing the kids.

They went to Trish's room first and he kissed her on the forehead. "I'm home, Trish. I just wanted to say goodnight."

Looking like an angel tucked under her covers, a big stuffed cougar wrapped in her arms, she didn't stir.

"I don't think she'll wake. Jeff will though."

"Night, Trish." Jack kissed her cheek, then he went in to see Jeff in his cowboy-decorated bedroom. Jack sat on the edge of the bed. "Hey, cowboy. Did you miss me?"

Jeff's eyes popped open and he stared at Jack as if trying to figure out who he was, then frowned. His eyes widened and he grabbed his dad in a hug. "Daddy! You came back."

"Yeah, but I might have to leave again soon. At least I was able to come home for tonight."

Jeff hugged him and wouldn't let go. Jack hugged him right back. It was heartwarming to feel loved and to love his child back. "I told Trish I was back but she didn't wake."

"Aww, she's always like that," Jeff said.

"Well, you need to get back to sleep and I'm going to bed now too."

"Where are you going to sleep? Wanna sleep with me? I can move over."

Jack smiled. "Mom and daddies sleep together. I'm going to bed with Mommy now."

"Okay." Jeff bit his lip. "If I get scared can I still go to Mommy's bed?"

"You bet. Night, son. Hope to see you for breakfast in the morning." Jack gave him another hug, covered Jeff up, and left with Dottie to go to the master bedroom.

"So what happened?"

Jack told her everything that they had learned.

She shook her head concerning the part that Mrs. Adkins said about Dottie wanting to be with Butch. "I doubt he wanted to see the kids or me. Why he returned was a complete mystery."

"You never know about people. Maybe he realized how good he'd had it. At least for me, I know."

"Thanks, Jack. The two of you are night and day."

They went to bed and though Jack loved his job, he was thinking just how much he'd love to be home nights after working a regular nine-to-five job.

CHAPTER 11

The next morning, Jack kissed Dottie on the cheek while they were waking up. He sure wished they could have a family day today. "I'm going to call Leyton and see what's up with this case. If we're sitting tight, I'll just have fun with the kids, and maybe your sitter can be available if I have to go in?"

Dottie smiled up at him and pulled him in for a hug. "That sounds nice. The kids will love it. They're doing preschool lessons, but they can skip a day to play with their daddy." She kissed him, then rolled out of bed to take a shower.

"You know, any time you want to quit the job, if you want to, I'd be happy."

She smiled at him. "I need to give two-week's notice at

least."

"Hot damn. We're going to celebrate."

She laughed. "All right. The kids will be thrilled. I'll let Dan know when I get in. Oh, wait, he's not going to be in for a couple of days."

"Why? Is he sick?"

"Personal business. Not that I'm saying there's anything to what our coffee shop owner says—she's our resident town gossip—but she said she saw a blond enter Dan's house as if she lived there. Dan wasn't home at the time."

"Huh." Jack smiled, tugging on a pair of clean boxer briefs. "Well, it makes for a nice bit of gossip, if nothing else."

"You haven't heard anything about what's going on with him, have you?"

Jack pulled Dottie back in for a hug. "Nope. I sure am glad you're going to be home so that anytime I'm off, we can spend the time together. I thought we could run as cougars tonight."

"I'd love that. You haven't had a chance to mark the territory."

He laughed. "Not the first thought I had. I wanted to get a feel of the surrounding woodlands out here. Then, yeah, I'll mark the territory, just in case anything wild has a notion to bother you and the kids."

"I need to shower. I hear Jeff up already."

"Okay, I'll throw on some clothes and fix them breakfast."

"Wow, this is really nice." Then she hurried to the bathroom to shower.

He finished getting dressed and headed into the kitchen, calling Leyton as he went to see what was on the schedule concerning Hellion. Jack hoped he had a break so he could spend the day with the kids. This would be great. A wonderful time to bond since he hadn't had a chance to in the past three months.

"Nothing," Leyton said. "We can't find any clue as to where they've gone to now. We're searching any place Ralph might have ended up so he could have someone take care of the bullet wounds. No word on that. We figure they'll deal with it themselves, and he'll be ready to go after a couple of days. For now, enjoy the time with the kids. I know you've been wanting to see them since you arrived home. Just have someone on call to take care of them if something happens and we need you. Travis is itching to go back to work with us, and is promising he won't get hit this time."

Jack chuckled. "Sounds good."

"Daddy!" Trish ran to give him a hug.

"I'll let you go. Sounds like you have some bonding to do."

"Thanks, Leyton,...for everything."

Then Jack ended the call and lifted Trish into his arms and carried her into the kitchen. Jeff was peering into the fridge, but when he saw Jack, Jeff ran to give him a hug too. "I told Trish you were here," he said. "She didn't believe me."

"I'm here and I'm going to fix breakfast. If I don't get called in, I'm going to stay with you for the whole day. Then when Mommy gets off from work, we're going for a cougar run."

"Yay!" both kids said and Jack put Trish down.

Jack peered into the fridge, then pulled out the carton of eggs. This was the first time ever for him to cook breakfast for the kids solo. "How about ham and cheese omelets?"

"Yeah!" Trish said.

Jeff nodded.

"What do you do when Mommy cooks?"

"Wash our hands." "Set the table." "Help with cooking."

Jack raised a brow. "All right. Wash your hands and I'll cut up the cheese and ham and you can put them on the eggs." He was sure his mother hadn't let him anywhere near the kitchen ever. Not until he had a place of his own and a girlfriend showed him how to cook. Not that his mother thought boys shouldn't cook. She just didn't want him making a mess in her kitchen. He guessed the time he tried to make a peanut butter and jelly sandwich had convinced her he wasn't a chef-in-the-making. He couldn't help it if she kept the peanut butter in the fridge and it wouldn't come off the butter knife easily. He supposed he should have looked a little harder for where the peanut butter that hadn't made it on his sandwich had ended up.

"Okay, so Mommy said you have schoolwork to do?" Jack helped them get situated at the kitchen counter so they could sprinkle the cheese and ham on the eggs.

"Yeah, Mommy and Abby have been teaching us." Trish pointed to a stack of papers and books.

"But we always eat first cuz we have to have brain food, Mommy says," Jeff added.

"Okay, brain food first, and then we'll do some work on your school assignments." Jack hadn't had preschool when he was a kid, so he wasn't even sure what they were supposed to be learning. He suspected that the materials would be easy enough to understand. "You can show me what you're supposed to be doing first. Then after we get some of our school work out of the way, we can do something outside for a while. Recess."

They looked at him like they didn't know what recess was. "We'll just go outside for some fresh air and sunshine. Maybe a hike."

As the kids helped, they dropped ham cubes and shredded cheese all over the floor and the island counter. He realized he should have made more just so they had some for the eggs.

He finished fixing them both ham and cheese omelets and served them up when Dottie joined him in the kitchen and kissed him. "Well, this is a lovely change for me." She glanced at the cheese and ham on the floor.

He quickly served her an omelet and a cup of coffee. "Okay, so the kids and I have our day cut out for us. When you get home, I'll fix dinner and then we can go for a cougar run. And don't worry about the mess. We'll clean it up."

"I'm sooo glad you're home, Jack."

"Me too," Trish said.

"Me too," Jeff echoed.

When Dottie was finished with breakfast, she gave each of the kids a hug, and then Jack. "You sure you're going to be okay?"

"Yep. We're going to have fun. Hey, how hard can this be?" Jack figured it would be a piece of cake compared to what he had to deal with as a CSF agent.

"I agree. Do what your daddy says and don't give him too hard a time."

"We won't," the kids both said.

"See you later, honey." He walked her out to the car. "I have all the emergency numbers if I need them."

"I called Abby and told her that she's on standby at a moment's notice."

"Okay, good show."

And then one more hug and kiss and Jack sent Dottie on her way. He cleaned up the plates and frying pan, while the kids swept up the mess they'd made on the floor. He helped go over it again. He asked the twins what they wanted to do first. He thought this was going to be a challenge, but they were used to a routine and both brought out papers that they used to draw lines from beginning letter sounds to pictures on a paper.

"Good," Jack said when both had perfect papers. "Now what?"

"We practice our ABC's." Trish ran to get their lined paper before Jeff could.

They wrote their A's in capital and lower case and while they were working on that, Jack called Shannon. "I was trying to figure out a good school break for the kids. Do you think swimming at the lake is too much?"

"No, Jack. That's perfect. Are you at home with the kids?"

"Yeah, the case is stymied for the moment. So Leyton said I could stay home with the kids. We're doing lessons and after that, I thought we could go swimming for a while, then return to finish up lessons."

"Remember they're only four. So they don't have an eight-hour day of class work."

"Uh, okay. Sounds good. If I get called up to chase bad guys, can you watch the kids until Abby can pick them up?"

"Absolutely. Get your beach towels, swim suits, and bring them over."

"Okay in a couple of hours."

He read to them, they read to him, practiced counting, and then they brought out their shapes and put them in the matching shape form, and used crayons to identify their colors.

After playing with money for a while, Jack was ready to take them swimming. He thought of taking them out for lunch afterward. He didn't want to suggest it in case they were tired after swimming. They both had fallen asleep in the car on the way home from the Renaissance fair and from the theme park, so he halfway expected it to happen after swimming too. After a night of loving Dottie, he'd be ready for a nap also.

"Ready to go swimming?"

"Yah!" Both kids ran off to get their swimsuits on and Jack dressed in his, then wore his jeans over that. So far, he'd had a great day. The kids had been having fun too.

When they arrived at Lake Buchanan, he let Shannon know they were there, and she came out with her two kids, both blue-eyed, blond, two-year-old girls, Sadie and Zoey. Tracey was visiting also and said she had to learn how to teach her twins how to swim after they were born and were the right age. She sat on a chair on the beach while Shannon and Jack took the kids to the water's edge.

"Now this is something you don't usually see. It's either all the guys, women, and kids, or just the women and kids. Certainly not Mr. Mom and kids," Tracey said, smiling.

Jack laughed and they took their inner tubes into the water. It was really nice and warm, and he thought how much fun it would be to swim as cougars here too, at night when the campers weren't about.

"Do they wear floaties?" he asked.

"Nope. Not as cats. We've been bringing them down here since they were infants," Shannon said.

That made him regret that he hadn't been doing this all along with the kids and Dottie. The kids were in the shallow water for a time, tossing a ball to him, and then they swam out to him, though he moved in closer to shore. He pulled them around on the inner tubes, and he figured he was getting great exercise while having a ball.

Then his cell rang.

"I'll get it," Tracey said, having a time getting out of the chair and finally pulling his cell from his jeans. "Hey, Dottie. Yeah, it's me. He brought the kids out to swim. Shannon's here too with her twins. He's doing great. They haven't drowned him yet." She laughed.

Jack smiled.

But then Tracey said, "Uh-oh."

He looked up from playing with the kids and saw water running down Tracey's legs.

"My water just broke."

Jack scooped up his kids and headed into shore. "I need to take Tracey to the hospital. She's having twins just like the two of you."

"Well, we know one's a boy. Could have two boys, or one boy and a girl," Tracey said. "Your hubby is taking me in. Don't worry about it. I'll give...Hal a call. Thanks."

"I'll dry and dress the kids," Shannon said, "if you can drive Tracey to the clinic."

"Okay."

"I'll just keep the kids until you get back."

"All right, thanks, Shannon."

"Thanks, Jack. Dottie, have to go," Tracey said, looking a little pale.

Jack grasped Tracey's arm and helped her to a chair on the deck. Then he dried off, dressed, and said goodbye to the kids. "I'll pick you up in a little bit and we'll have lunch. The babies could take hours before they're born. But their daddy will stay with their mommy."

"Okay," Jeff said.

Tracey was already on her phone to call Hal. "My water broke. Yes, but don't kill yourself getting to the clinic, Hal. Jack is driving me. He and the kids and Shannon and hers were swimming at the lake. I came over to visit. Shannon will watch all the kids. All you have to do is meet me at the clinic."

Jack helped her out to his car.

"Wait. I'll ask." Tracey turned to Jack. "Hal wants to know: can you deliver a baby? Well, two. Just in case?"

CHAPTER 12

Dottie wasn't sure who was more panicked about Tracey's water breaking: Daddy Hal, Jack, who was on the way to the clinic to take Tracey to see the doctor, or Dottie, who was always level-headed in a crisis. Then she figured if Jack could handle this, he could handle the situation with her when the time came.

Jack got on his car phone, calling in to Dottie. "The babies are coming. Right. Now. We have to pull over and park."

Omigod, Dottie couldn't believe poor Tracey was having the babies before she reached the clinic. And that poor Jack was stuck dealing with it.

"Okay, can you help her strip out of her clothes so she

can shift into a cougar? That will be easier. Stryker is on his way to help out. Hal is too far out to reach you in time. Chase is on a call and two hours away. So you're it until Stryker gets there."

"I found a place to pull over. We're only about a quarter mile down the road from the cabins. I'll leave the line open while I help Tracey." He helped get her out of the front seat. "Sorry, Tracey. We're not going to make it."

"No problem," she gritted out, clutching her belly.

"Okay, I'm going to help you strip out of your clothes, then you can shift. Can you do that for me?"

She nodded and sat down on the edge of the back seat. He took off her sandals, helped her to stand, and pulled down her shorts and panties. He tossed them on the floor because they were all wet. Then he pulled up her shirt, and unfastened her bra. Cougars often saw other cougars naked when they shifted, but even so, he was new to the neighborhood, hadn't even met Tracey before, and he hoped she wasn't uncomfortable about this.

Then he figured she was in too much pain, and the babies were coming anytime now, so nothing else really mattered. "Okay, let me spread the couple of blankets on the—"

"We're cougars. Just spread them on the ground. I'll have them there. No sense in making a mess of your car."

"Okay." He spread them out on the ground and helped her to the blanket, hoping she could shift. Sometimes when they were in a lot of pain, shifters had trouble shifting either way.

"Call Hal and tell him I'll be there *after* the delivery."

"Okay." But Jack wasn't calling anyone. Not while he was trying to help deliver the twins.

Then she shifted into a beautiful, golden cougar and lay panting on the blanket. He hollered to his car phone, the doors to the car still open, the Bluetooth still on. "We're having the babies as cougars. We can't make it to the clinic. We're doing fine." At least he sure the hell hoped so. And he was damn glad as shifters they could have babies either way, particularly when it came to more complicated multiple births.

"I've already alerted the paramedics. They'll be at your location in twenty minutes," Dottie said.

Jack looked at Tracey, her green eyes on him. She shook her head and the next thing he knew, she was pushing out the first wet, spotted kitten. She turned and cleaned up the baby and it made its way to her belly to suckle. The baby looked to be about a pound in size, so normal. She laid down again and panted. He wondered how long it would take to have the second kitten. Ten minutes later, it was born. She did the same with the second cub, cleaned it up, and then the cub found its way to momma's milk.

It was a miracle to see the birth and he was glad Tracey instinctively knew what to do as a cougar. He thought he should move her to the car now. Then again, maybe he should wait for the paramedics. They could use a stretcher to lift her and it would be easier for her to recline on a gurney. Plus, a paramedic would be in the back with her and the cubs to watch over them while the other one drove.

He went to the car and said, "Hey, Dottie, Tracey had her twins. Should I put her in the car and bring her in, or wait for the paramedics?"

"Wait for—"

He heard the siren then. "Yeah, they're nearly here. We'll wait. Tell Hal, mom and cubs are doing great. Wait..." He saw Tracey leaning down again as if she'd just had another cub, and he laughed. "Hell, tell Hal he has triplets."

***

Since Hal was Dan's deputy sheriff, Dottie had to tell Dan that Tracey's babies—triplets—had come, just to give him a heads up. She hated bothering him when he had "personal business" to take care of, but he would be upset with her if she left him out of the loop.

"Hal and Tracey just had triplets," she told Dan.

"Triplets? I thought they were having twins."

"Yeah, sorry to have to disturb you if you were busy"— with a blond, Dottie was thinking—"but Jack had to help deliver her on the way to the clinic. Everyone's fine." She was glad Jack hadn't panicked. "You don't need to do anything. Everything's under control. I just wanted you to know Hal was going to be off the job for a little while in case he was needed as a deputy sheriff."

"Thanks, Dottie. If everything is under control, I'll check in at the clinic in a couple of days."

Dottie really thought something was up now. Dan would have been down there with the rest of them, annoying Kate as she tried to take care of Mom and babies.

"Okay, just wanted to…let you know. I need to get back to work."

"Okay, thanks for letting me know." Then Dan hung up.

Dottie just stared at the phone. "Okay, Dan. What is going on with you?" She called Shannon to let her know that Jack had delivered the cubs—triplets—on the road just fine

TERRY SPEAR

and that they'd need to do another baby shower for her—for baby number three.

She got a beep that Jack was calling in again, and she quickly ended the call with Shannon, worried something was wrong. "What's up, Jack?"

"Make that quadruplets. Ensure that when someone tells Hal he has four cubs instead of three, he's sitting down."

***

As soon as Tracey was on her way to the clinic with her four cubs, Jack returned to pick up Jeff and Trish and thanked Shannon for looking after them.

Shannon was shaking her head at the notion that Tracey had double the kids from what the doc could hear, heartbeat-wise. "Quadruplets." She chuckled. "Hal's going to need some extra help. Good thing they have a large ranch house. I don't think their foreman or the two ranch hands, Ricky and Kolby Jones, will want babysitting duty though. Then again, Hal's parents, Roger and Millie, and Hal's sister, Allie, will help out. Not to mention that they own and run the town newspaper. It will be front page news."

Jack laughed. "We're going to see if we can pick up some lunch for Dottie."

"You're so good for her. You've only been here for a

240

couple of days and already you've made a big impact on all of us—in a great way. Thanks for taking care of Tracey."

"I'm glad I was here to help." Jack loaded the kids in the car and Jeff said, "I'm hungry."

"We'll call your mom at the sheriff's office and find out what she would like to eat, and we'll pick up something for all of us."

Jack said bye to Shannon and then he climbed into the car and called Dottie on the way back into town. He spied a cougar running in the woods and Trish said, "That's Mr.Kretchen. He runs all the time."

Jack guessed he was a little on edge about Hellion and his gang, thinking anytime he saw an unfamiliar cougar, which would be everyone in town, practically, he would worry it was Hellion or one of his cohorts.

"Hey, Dottie, we're on our way back from the lake. Can we swing by and bring you lunch and eat ours with you??"

"Oh, absolutely! How fun that will be. I'd love a grilled ham and cheese."

He was glad he could make her day. "You got it."

"Were you able to take the kids swimming before all the excitement?"

"We did. Kids are getting really good about diving for

toys in the water. I wasn't sure they were old enough to do that."

"Yeah, everyone's been teaching them."

"They're doing a great job. We'll be there with lunch in half an hour or a little longer."

"Thanks, Jack. See you soon."

Jack had a call from Hal then and hoped he wasn't upset with Jack over anything concerning his wife's delivery.

"I owe you, Jack. Hell, I didn't know what to think about you. I'm damn glad you're here and helping Dottie, the kids, and the rest of us out when we need assistance."

"I'm glad to help. How's she doing?"

"Still in her cougar form. Resting while the cubs are nursing. Lots easier to nurse four cubs than four hungry babies. Anyway, I just wanted to tell you if you ever need anything, don't hesitate to call me."

"Daddy needs to learn how to ride a horse," Jeff hollered from the back seat.

Jack laughed. It seemed he wasn't getting out of that, no matter what. "Yeah, I guess lessons on how to ride a horse would be good when we can spare the time."

Hal chuckled. "No problem. I have two great ranch hands and a foreman who would love to teach you."

"So Daddy can be a knight," Jeff said.

"Thanks. I'll take you up on it when things aren't so hectic."

"Good deal. Well, have to go back in and check on the missus. Talk later."

When they ended the call, Jack asked the kids, "Do you know where they have grilled ham and cheese sandwiches?"

"No." "Nope."

Jack called Dottie back. "Hey, one other thing. Where can I get the lunches?"

He picked up hot dogs and grilled ham and cheese sandwiches, which appealed to him right after she'd mentioned them, for both Dottie and him. When they joined her for lunch, she had a couple of calls, and then began to eat her sandwich.

"This is so good. I haven't had one of these in eons," Dottie said.

"Me either," Trish said.

Jack agreed.

"We're going to have to have another baby shower for Tracey." Dottie sipped some of her pink lemonade. She received another call concerning Tracey. "Yes, she had quadruplets and Jack was there when she delivered them.

Two boys and two girls. Yes. Everyone is just fine. Hal?" She laughed. "Him too. Yes, another baby shower. We'll let everyone know once we learn who wants to organize it. Okay, that would be great. Thanks."

Jack smiled at Dottie.

"Mrs. Fitzgerald. I've been fielding calls since you were there for Tracey's delivery. Finally, Mrs. Fitzgerald heard the news at the coffee shop, and she'll tell the rest of the town and organize the baby shower."

"Since Hal's unable to perform as a deputy sheriff, Chase is out on an assignment, and Dan's still out on personal business, if Stryker needs any help, he can just call me."

"I'll tell him. He'll appreciate it. He's had to deal with a two-car collision, a black bear wandering through town, two cat-in-tree calls from the same woman, and the issue of a stolen bike. Which turns out the owner just forgot where he parked it. So far, that's it."

"Okay good."

"So what did you do today?" Dottie asked the kids.

They told her about doing their lessons and swimming and then Tracey's bag breaking and their daddy taking her to the clinic to have all her babies.

"We're going to play when we get home," Trish said.

"Hal is going to teach Daddy to ride a horse," Jeff said.

Dottie smiled at Jack. "I think you're finally being accepted into the town."

After they ate, Jack and the kids went home and would see Dottie in three more hours. The house was warm and comfortable. The kind of place that had a feel-good aura the first time he had walked in the door. Bookcases sat on either side of a stone fireplace, and were filled with books, both educational about the flora, fauna, maps of the world, and romance novels, but children's fantasy books, board games, and the kids' school books were there too. A book on naming babies caught his attention.

Jack thought again about what had happened to Tracey, delivering her babies, and learning there were four and not only two. He wondered if they would discover something similar when Dottie gave birth too.

***

When the kids were in bed that night, Jack was enjoying sitting on the velvety blue and beige striped couch with Dottie, watching a show. He reached over and ran his hand over her belly. "You don't think we're going to have any surprises, do you?"

"I figure the further along we are, the better chance of

knowing. I talked to Tracey and she said she was still so small and the heartbeats of two of the babies were in sync with the other two that it appeared she was carrying only twins. I should know by next week if I'm having twins though."

"Okay."

She kissed him on the mouth. Then she stood and said, "Let's take this to the bedroom." She knew where they were headed and didn't want to get all worked up and then have to quit and take it to the privacy of their bedroom. If they didn't have kids already, no problem.

Before they reached the bedroom, Jack's phone rang, and he pulled it out of his pocket. "It's Leyton calling. Have to take this."

They retired to the bedroom and Dottie suspected that if Leyton was calling now, it was important. But did it mean Jack had to run, or was it just an update and he could stay the night?

"All right. I'll be over there in fifteen." Jack ended the call and joined Dottie, pulling her into his arms. "Leyton received word that Hellion and the gang are two hours west of here. Travis and Bridget are going with us and we're going to try and take them down."

"Let me know you're okay when you get there. It doesn't

matter what time of night. Just call me. All right?"

"You bet. I have to go. We don't want them to get away this time." He kissed her and then she walked with him out to the car.

"Keep yourself and the others safe."

"Will do."

Dottie realized, as she waved Jack goodbye, this job could get him killed every bit as much as when he was on active duty with the army, far away from home. Well, on training missions even. Yet, she also figured Jack needed to do this kind of work to feel a sense of accomplishment. From what Kate told him, Leyton said Jack was already a topnotch agent. So he seemed perfectly suited to the job. At least she'd had last night with him, and the kids had spent all day bonding with their daddy and that was important.

About four hours later, Dottie was in bed, trying to sleep, when she received a call from Jack. "They were at a hotel. We found blood on some bandages on the bathroom counter in the room where they were staying. They'd packed up and moved on. This is completely a cat-chasing-the-dirty-rat game. We're unable to determine where they've gone to next."

"Did they leave shortly before you arrived, or has it been

some time?"

"We'd say, from their scents, about two hours."

"So about the time you learned they were there."

"Yeah."

"Sounds almost like someone tipped them off."

"Yeah, that's exactly what we're thinking. We've let Chuck know since his informant gave him the information. If the guy is in on this with Hellion, he'll be next on our list. The only good thing is we know his information was good. We just need to get it before they take off again."

"So what are you going to do?"

"We're going to get a place for the night and wait until we have further word. Is everything okay there?"

"Yeah, thanks. I was just waiting to hear from you. Now I can go to sleep."

"All right. Night, Dottie. Pleasant dreams."

"Night. If you head out, let me know, okay?"

"You need to sleep."

"Call me."

"All right." Jack chuckled. "Night, honey."

"Night, Jack." And then Dottie settled down to sleep.

When the morning came, she realized Jack hadn't called her. She assumed they still were just waiting for word as to where to go next. She made breakfast for the kids, and was really looking forward to not working, and being home with them. And being home with Jack when he could be here with them.

After Abby arrived, Dottie went into work and her first call was from Mrs. Fitzgerald. "Oh, Dottie, I don't know what's going on with Dan. Dr. Kate had to make an emergency call to his house last night. I thought you should know if he hasn't told you what the trouble is, just in case you need to offer assistance."

What in the world was going on? "Does the woman who is visiting him have a car?"

"No. She was driving his. Then she just walked into his house and closed the door. He wasn't even there."

"Did she look injured? Like she was limping or anything?"

"She looked fine. From what I could tell. She was close to the door and went inside, and I was driving by at the time so I had to keep driving. Plus, it was dark out, so hard to tell. Except I could see she was a blond."

"Okay, thanks." Dottie really didn't want to ask Dan about this. If it was something private, Kate wouldn't explain what was going on. And the same with Dan. Given all the secrecy, it had to be. Was Dan hurt? She bit her lip. If he was hurt, she felt it was her duty to check on him.

CHAPTER 13

That morning at work, Dottie had to call Stryker about a cougar who had been speeding in town. "Uhm, one other thing. According to Mrs. Fitzgerald, Dr. Kate had to make a house call. Now, I'm not prying or anything, but it had me worried. Do you know if Dan's all right? Or the woman? Kate rarely, if ever, makes house calls."

"Hell, I don't know."

"Okay. Have a call. Need to go." Dottie picked up the call from her babysitter, Abby. Dottie was worried something had happened to one of the twins. "Is everything okay?"

"You wanted the kids and me to plant some green beans and tomato plants so they can take care of their very own little garden. I picked up the bigger variety of tomato plants and I began digging in the garden that you never use. And I found a metal container. Just the top of it. At first, I thought it was a rock. But it's metal. It's covered in a plastic sack, probably so it wouldn't rust. I didn't uncover it any further. Just in case you buried it there. Do you want me to leave it alone?"

"Can you find another spot to dig in? Just leave that alone for now?"

"Sure. Did you want me to rebury this?"

"No, just leave it. I'll take a look at it when I get home."

"All right. Trish and Jeff are excited about planting. They're both digging away at a spot about five feet away."

"I found one too!" Jeff called out.

"Another metal box?" Dottie couldn't believe it. She hadn't been gardening in that area. Dottie wanted to create a real children's garden like she had when she was a girl, and she thought it would be a lot of fun for them. There was only one person she could think of that would be planting metal boxes in her backyard. Jeffrey. What had he hidden on the property? But why wouldn't he have come back for it before he was killed?

"Okay, I can't leave work. I'll call Stryker to drop by there and dig them up and check them out." Dottie didn't want to risk that Jeffrey had hidden explosives or something else in the boxes that could be dangerous. "Just don't touch them in case there's something dangerous in them."

"I guess we need to plant later then."

"Awww," Trish and Jeff said.

"Your momma's worried something bad is in them. Uncle Stryker will take a look at them." Abby said to Dottie, "I'll move the plants under the patio for shade. It's snack time anyway."

"Okay, I'll call Stryker."

"Thanks."

Dottie called Stryker at once. "Hey, Abby and the kids were going to start a garden just for them. They found two metal boxes buried in plastic sacks in the ground."

"I'm on my way over."

"Thanks. I told them to just leave them there in case anything unsafe is inside."

"Good idea. I'll let you know as soon as I know anything."

"I'm going to call Jack on this too, since they're trying to run down these men."

"Sounds good."

When Dottie called Jack, he was really concerned. "I'll let Leyton know. We need to learn just what is in the containers in case it gives us any clues. If Hellion is aware of the buried boxes, he and his cohorts might even head that way."

"I don't understand why Jeffrey wouldn't have come back for it, unless it was something better left buried."

Jack talked to Leyton in the background. "Abby found metal boxes buried in the backyard. Dottie suspects Jeffrey buried them there. Stryker's on his way to check them out."

"Tell Dottie we're on our way. We can't risk that there may be something important in the boxes, that Hellion knows about them, and might end up there. Abby needs to take the kids to Hal's place. While Hal's busy with Tracey and the babies, their ranch hands can watch out for them since Chase is out of town."

"Okay. Did you hear that, Dottie?"

"Yeah. I'm calling Abby now."

"All right. We'll be there in about two hours. Leyton says I'm to stay there once I'm home. Just in case."

"Can they take care of the perps without you?"

"They said they can. They don't want to risk that Hellion or any of the others might visit our place when someone's not there to offer protection for you and the kids. But they also need to stop them if they do end up there. I'll be glad to be home, watching out for you. I might have to have you and the kids stay at Hal's place for a while. Just in case."

"We'll see." Dottie didn't want to stay out there. The kids were another story. She wouldn't risk their safety if there was any chance Hellion and the others were going to her place. "Stryker's calling me. I'll put this on conference call. Yes, Stryker, what did you find?"

"Three metal containers filled with three-hundred thousand dollars in cash."

Shocked, Dottie gasped.

"So far. And here's the thing. Some of those bills are only a couple of years old and they have Jeffrey's scent on them."

"Meaning Jeffrey had to have planted them there more recently. Omigod." She felt chills chase up her spine. "Is there any chance they're counterfeit?"

"Nope. I'd say that he's been coming here for some time, and depositing the cash when he knew you weren't around. There are more containers. I called Dan to let him know."

"Don't tell me. You're taking care of it and he's fine with it."

"Yeah. That's right. If anything significant happens though, he'll come in. I need to keep digging to make sure there are no more containers than the one I'm working on now."

"We'll be there in about an hour and a half," Jack said, "If the way Leyton is speeding is any indication."

"Just tell him we want you all home in one piece," Dottie warned.

She was busy with minor calls to the sheriff's department after that. She had to tell everyone Stryker was the only one available right now, but that he was off on an important mission. Until some of the CSF agents arrived to take over, he'd be delayed.

By the time Jack and Leyton arrived at her home, Stryker had uncovered ten metal boxes full of cash. He'd been too busy digging it up to count it yet. She was so angry at Jeffrey, if he hadn't been dead, she could have killed him. He put her and the kids at risk hiding all that money in her yard—if anyone had learned of it and wanted to get rid of them so he could easily steal the money.

"Hey, Dottie, we're going to be digging up more of the old garden patch, looking for anything else that might be here," Jack said. "Stryker's calling you as soon as he's done so he can take care of the other calls that came in while he was out back digging. He's in the house washing up. We'll count the money and then we can take it to the bank. It's your money, though."

"Wait, won't depositing that much cash trigger an investigation?"

"You'll put what you need in savings, and then everything else can go in safe deposit boxes."

Dottie let out her breath. "We should use it for the good of the community. I know we can't report it to anyone, because then there would be an investigation into what had happened to him. We can't have that kind of trouble for the cougar town."

"The bank's cougar run. They'll keep this quiet and under wraps. You keep what you need, and use the rest for whatever you deem appropriate. It's your money, finders, keepers—all of it found on your property," Jack said.

"Ours."

"Okay, well, it's yours to do with what you wish."

"I want to pay off the house mortgage first, and keep some for renovating the house so we'll have more room for the new baby. But the rest—well, we can talk to everyone and see what might benefit the most."

"I'd just be careful about mentioning where the money came from," Leyton said.

"Anonymous donor."

Leyton said, "That works."

When she got off work, she called Jack. "Is it all right to bring the kids home from Hal's? Ted took them riding, and they saw the babies, but they want to come home now."

"Yeah. I already called them to tell them we were coming to get them. They said no problem. Ricky's bringing the kids to the house. He should be here in another twenty minutes. About the time you get home."

"Thanks, Jack." She couldn't believe how he could do what normally only she could do with the kids. She would have to get used to that, and was happy to do so.

When she arrived home, the kids, eating snacks of peanut butter crackers and slices of peaches, greeted her. "Daddy and Uncle Leyton are out in the backyard filling up the holes to make it nice and neat like it was before," Jeff said.

"That's good." She ruffled his hair.

"They put the play money in the kitchen," Trish said. "But they told us we couldn't count it because it's too big."

Dottie went inside the house and when she saw the bundles of $100 bills in the amount of $10,000 each stacked on the island counter, she couldn't believe it. She felt like she was looking at a bank vault full of cash, except it was sitting in her very unsecure kitchen. She just stared at the bills as the kids told her about riding the ponies and seeing the babies.

She finally glanced at the kids. "Did they name them?"

"Not yet. Uncle Hal said there were too many of them and they had to go back to the drawing board," Trish said.

Dottie laughed. She peeked out the big kitchen window and saw Jack and Leyton smoothing out the areas that had been dug up. Stryker was already back on his job as deputy sheriff, answering the myriad minor calls. She was thinking there might be a couple of hundred thousand that they'd dug up, so not that much money. So once she paid her mortgage off, and then did some remodeling on the house, she didn't figure there'd be much left over. Boy, was she ever shocked to learn how much more there was.

Doing the math, there had to be close to three and a half million dollars stacked on her counter. She sat down hard on her bar stool, feeling numb all over.

Trish said, "Mommy, Daddy said we were going to have pizza to celebrate."

"Sounds good. I'm thinking that's his favorite food to eat." Dottie wondered what they were going to do with all of this money.

Jack came into the house and pulled Dottie into his arms and gave her a big kiss. "We tried to straighten it up out there. So did you count it?"

"About three and a half million."

"Have you figured out what to spend it all on?"

"The mortgage, some remodeling, redecorating." She'd been squeaking by with her worn out hand-me-downs and the place needed new carpeting, paint, tile work. Just a lot of stuff. "And then some things for the community. Hiking and biking trails all over the area. Maybe a children's garden. We were going to make one here, but it would be fun to do that and have a bigger one for kids in the community. Ponds with koi, fountains, ducks, egrets, so they'll have wildlife too. Some fun things for the kids to climb on like giant turtles and little bridges to cross over waterways. But the kids would have their very own vegetable and flower gardens there too."

"Which could be great for teaching them too, since everyone homeschools their kids," Jack said.

"Right. Maybe we could spruce up the center of town— make a plaza with a fountain and flowers."

"Sounds good to me," Leyton said as he came inside.

"So what do we do now with the money?" Dottie asked.

"Thanks to the fact that cougars run everything in town, including the bank, that won't be a problem. Stryker said he'd return to help escort you to the bank with the money. We'll help get it there instead," Leyton said. "We're all armed and no one would dare try to take it from any of us."

"We still can't just deposit it all in our account." She realized she needed to get Jack's name on her account. They were married now, so everything needed to be in both their names, the house included. "The bank would have to report all that money to make sure it wasn't ill-gotten gains."

"Right, if it wasn't a cougar-run bank. Cash of three-thousand dollars or over can cause the bank manager to question it. In our bank's case, no. The bank's president, Rick Mueller, and his wife, Yvonne, the investment broker at the bank, both are former FBI agents and he had been Special Forces, will take care of this. Now, that's still too much money to deposit at one time though," Leyton said. "So you can put it in several safe deposit boxes for the remainder. In most banks, they don't allow cash to be saved in the boxes because thefts have occurred at banks and the contents can't be verified or insured. But at our bank, no problem. Even so, there are three CSF agents, yourself, and one deputy sheriff who all know how much will be stored there. And then just spend it as you need to for the various projects."

"Another idea is to put a big chunk of that money into investments, and then the money will create more income and can continue to be used, not just for a one-time affair," Jack said.

"Now I like that idea. Then it can continue to fund projects for the community. I guess we need to get this over to the bank now." It was making Dottie nervous to see that much money sitting in her kitchen. "What did you do with the metal containers?"

"We thought of just burying them again. If you want to plant in that garden spot, they would be in the way of the new roots. Stryker took them with him to dispose of," Jack said. "I've already called the bank to tell the manager that we have some cash coming in, and we'll need to get several of the bigger safe deposit boxes."

"Okay, I guess this will all fit into a couple of suitcases, and we can just roll it into the bank. I'll go get them." Dottie returned with her largest bags and the guys all filled them up for her. She was looking forward to getting with key people in the community and seeing what everyone wanted to do. That would be perfect when she quit her job, and she could be home with the kids and Jack still, whenever he was able to be around.

"What I don't understand is why Jeffrey was trying to get you to Kate's house that day," Leyton said, still sounding angry about it. "Jeffrey was threatening to kill Kate and he had every intention of killing me if he could have."

"What if he just wanted to make sure we weren't at the house so Bishop or Curly Joe, his partners at the time, could dig up the cash? There was practically always someone at the house. Maybe he was afraid they'd get caught, and he really didn't want me or the kids to get hurt."

"Yeah, Hal was over there watching Dottie. If she had left the house with the kids to see Kate, he would have gone with her and the house would have been empty. Since she lives out a ways from town, no one would have been the wiser," Leyton said.

"Hellion must not have known about the money. If Bishop had known about it, he was in jail so he couldn't go back out to Dottie's place and dig it up. Curly Joe was already dead. If Bishop knew about it, I can see why he didn't tell Hellion about the cash. He must have told them about the weapons so that Hellion would be partners with him, but he was afraid to let him in on the cash. Bishop probably assumed he'd get to it when he could. Maybe sell the weapons first," Leyton said.

Jack agreed. "And he'd need some muscle backup in his line of work. He couldn't just sell the arms without having someone watch his back."

"Only they cut him out of the deal. Forget backing him." Dottie shook her head. "No honor among thieves."

"Well, it's really a cutthroat business when it comes to money." Jack rolled one of the suitcases out to the car. Leyton grabbed the other.

Dottie secured the kids in the car and then Leyton followed in his car.

"I'm sure glad to be home," Jack said. "As soon as we learned Stryker had found so much money in the backyard, I wanted to be here for you, just in case Hellion or the others learned of it."

"So they're on call and will leave, but you're stuck staying with me and the kids?"

Jack laughed. "Best deal ever. The other way to handle this is for you and the kids to leave. Either go and stay with my parents, your aunt, or someone locally. I'm comfortable with anything as long as you and the kids aren't alone."

"I don't want to have to always run away or go into

hiding. We stay with you. I know how to shoot a gun and I have one of my own. I've taught the kids to hide under my bed and stay there until someone they know says it's all right to come out. Unless they smell smoke, and then they're to slip out into the woods and wait for me or someone they know."

"I'm sorry you've had to go through this, Dottie. You shouldn't have to."

"I agree. You were fighting in a war zone. And it's relatively safe here. I just hooked up with the wrong sort of man."

"Not this time."

She sighed. "No, you're wonderful for us."

"I just don't want you or the kids in any kind of danger."

"We could be anywhere we stay and then maybe put those we're staying with at risk too. I've been meaning to ask you about putting our names on both bank accounts and the house and anything else we need to."

"My thought also. I'll be getting direct deposit from work, so I'll need to set that up here." Jack wasn't sure everyone would warm up to him right away. Not when he was a newcomer, but when they arrived at the bank, the Muellers greeted him like he was a long lost friend.

"He's a keeper," Yvonne said, winking at Dottie.

Dottie blushed. "Yes, he is."

One of the loan officers took the kids back into a playroom where two other bank customers working on loans had their young children who appeared to be about six years old, both girls. They were working on puzzles and Jeff and Trish went in to help them.

Jack was glad that the bank was so family friendly since they were going to be here for a while. Rick took Jack and Dottie back to his office where he pulled the blinds to his windows that viewed the inside of the bank, offered them seats, and coffee, water, or sodas.

Once they had mugs of coffee, Rick called his wife in.

Yvonne joined them and told them how they could handle the investments. And then they did all the other banking they needed to do—adding Jack to the account, transferring money from his old one, signing up for direct deposit, and then finally opening some safe deposit boxes to keep the money secure until they needed it for projects.

"This is so good," Yvonne said. "Taking a criminal's money and using it for the good of our kind."

"He probably would have had a stroke if he'd known what we plan to do with his money."

"Maybe he'd buried it there for you and the kids," Yvonne said.

Dottie laughed. "If he had, why not mention it? No. He hid it for his own safekeeping. By doing so, he put us at further risk in the event any of his partners had come looking for it. I'm glad we can do some good with it."

After that, they went home for pizza. Stryker and Leyton also had a bite. Before Leyton headed home to his mate, Stryker received a call. "Yeah?" He looked at Dottie. "All right. Be right in." He hung up the phone and said, "Well, that was Kate. She said her patient, the caracal? She escaped. I have to run in and see if I can track her down."

"Boy, if she doesn't sound like Shannon." Dottie and Jack saw the guys out to their cars.

"Yeah, I missed Shannon's case. Who would ever have thought we'd have another I could be involved in like that." Then Stryker climbed into his car, waved goodbye, and headed back into town.

Leyton told Jack to call him if they had any trouble, and then he went home.

When Jack and Dottie returned to the house, Jeff said, "Uncle Ted asked when you're going to take riding lessons."

Jack knew that would come up until he did the

obligatory lessons. "How about tomorrow, if he can manage. While Mom's at work, we can go out there and ride horses."

Dottie smiled at Jack. "If you do a lot of riding, you'll be sore."

He took that as a hint that making love to her could be hard on him. "Won't stop me."

She laughed. "Insatiable. I know it."

CHAPTER 14

Dan finally showed up at the sheriff's department the next day and was all business. Quieter than usual. Busy.

When he had a free moment and was just staring out the window of his office, Dottie rapped on the door jamb and said, "Dan, Jack and I discussed me resigning from the position so I could be home for the new baby, for the twins, and for Jack when he's around." She wanted to give Dan the news early. She didn't want him to feel like she had to leave at a moment's notice.

"Sounds good."

"I thought I'd give two weeks' notice, unless you needed me for longer in the event that you couldn't get a replacement right away."

"Figuring now that you have a husband and another

baby on the way that you'd want to be home with your family, I already have it covered."

"Oh. Okay, well, good." She really was glad she wasn't leaving him, or the town, in a lurch, but she was surprised he was already making arrangements for her to be gone when she hadn't really decided much one way or another beforehand. He must have been able to read her better than she'd been able to read herself. She truly did want to be home with her family until the kids were older at least. Still, she wanted to talk to him about what was going on at home with him.

She walked into his office and shut the door. She had never felt nervous about discussing anything with him before. He seemed so distant, it was like an alien Dan had replaced the friend and boss she knew. "Is anything wrong?" She wouldn't have ever brought up the blond, but the situation with Kate making a house call continued to nag at her.

Dan's brows rose. "Why do you ask?"

"Well, you know Mrs. Fitzgerald."

He gave a dark, little chuckle. "And?" He leaned back in his chair, arms folded across his chest.

"She saw a blond enter your house when you weren't

there. And then Dr. Kate made a house call."

"Okay, listen, I'm not going to make up a story."

Waiting to hear the real story, Dottie barely breathed.

"But I can't tell you what's really going on. Neither can Kate. People could die. Suffice it to say, whatever Mrs. Fitzgerald wants to speculate about the situation, it's out of my hands."

"Okay. Thanks, Dan, for being honest with me."

That earned her a genuine smile, and she knew then everything was right with the world—at least between them. Whatever was going on with him was no one's business, and she knew when he was ready, he'd share.

***

For two weeks, the CSF agents hadn't been able to locate Hellion and his partners. Bridget and Travis had even flown out to Missouri, to ensure Hellion and Gigi hadn't returned there. Jack had been Mr. Mom and seemed fine with the role for now until he had another mission to go on, while he watched over the kids for the time Dottie had left at work. All of them delighted in having him home. Stryker had never located the unusual cat that had escaped Kate's clinic and left Yuma Town. Tracey and Hal had decided on names for their four babies with help from their cougar friends:

Tabitha, Evan, Denise, and Liam. Great names for darling babies.

Dan had jumped right back into his work, giving her a parting celebration for a job well-done, and everyone came by on her last day of work. She'd halfway expected him to replace her with a blond. The woman, who took Dottie's job as police dispatcher, was in her mid-thirties, had a ten-year-old boy, and a husband who worked as a reporter for the local paper. True to his word, Dan hadn't said a word about the blond, though everyone in Yuma Town had heard about it. He seemed so quiet about that, Dottie was afraid the woman had left him, and he'd been upset.

As to quitting her job, Dottie had worried she might get bored. She'd had no time for that. Between having fun with Jack and the kids, and coming up with plans for things the community could enjoy, she was having a ball at the beginning of her first week of no work. Not to mention they were in the middle of renovating the house so they could be ready for the new baby. And she had just finalized the plans for the wedding.

She suspected she was having twins again since she was about the same size at this stage in the pregnancy as the last time.

They had all gone over to Hal's ranch for Jack's second lesson at riding before Dottie had her doctor's appointment. Jeff and Trish were so excited about showing Jack how to ride a horse, she wasn't sure Ted would get a word in edgewise.

When they arrived at the ranch, Jack was wearing his cowboy boots, and he had a cowboy hat, jeans, and a western shirt already, so he looked the part. But when he stood next to Lucy, he looked a little unsure of himself.

"You gotta put your foot in the stirrup," Jeff said, "like you did before." Then he looked at Ted as if to make sure he'd said it right.

Ted was smiling, his arms folded across his chest, and he nodded. "Only way to ride is to just get on up there and...ride. A few more times and you'll be a pro."

"He's going to be a knight and fight the bad knight," Jeff said, as if anyone might have forgotten.

Jack ruffled Jeff's hair. "You're right. And a knight has to ride a horse." He mounted Lucy, and Ted reminded him how to balance himself in the saddle so he was riding in harmony with the horse, how to hold the reins, how to signal to her which way he wanted to go, how to signal to make her go, and how to signal her to stop, since it had been a couple of weeks since the first lesson and they hadn't been at it for very long.

Ted helped the kids on the ponies they always rode—Tippy and Talia—and then the three of them walked their horses around a yard while Dottie sat on a chair and watched them.

"Your kids are doing great," Ted said. "And after a few lessons, Jack will have this down. Now as to jousting, he'll need a lot more time in the saddle or he won't stay in it after the first round."

Dottie laughed. "He's our knight even if he's not jousting." Unfortunately, the kind of work he did was just as dangerous. But at least he knew how to do it.

***

Jack had to admit he felt a little foolish being such a newbie at this. He hadn't taken up any new activities in so long that everything he did was something he'd practiced at for years. So he had to keep telling himself this was his second horse ride ever and if he kept at it, he'd get really good at it. In fact, he was thinking that he wouldn't mind buying horses for the family, renting out space here at the ranch, and giving the kids the chance to really help raise their own horses. He'd ask Dottie first. Of course, that meant they would have a whole herd of horses at Hal's ranch once the new baby was old enough to ride.

He smiled at the thought—riding off on picnics, camping out, riding on horse trails, just all kinds of family activities that they could do around riding. But also, they could do things with the others who rode horses, big gatherings. It could be fun.

Someday, he supposed, he'd have to get a knight's costume to wear at Renaissance fairs when he took the family, and even around here, if the kids wanted to dress up for a ride like that.

Jeff and Trish looked so comfortable on their ponies, he was glad that Ted and the other ranch hands had been so good with teaching them. When Dottie was able to ride again, he would love for the family to do this together.

When Jack and the kids came in from riding, he realized his butt was sore, and he felt a little unsettled as he was walking on the ground. He figured the more he rode the horse, the more used to it he would get. He did love it, and was glad the horses had been raised by cougars and weren't afraid of the shifter kind.

"Thanks so much for the second lesson. I'll come back when I can," Jack said, "and bring the kids." He wasn't sure how long it would be before Dottie felt too uncomfortable seated in a chair at the ranch while he and the kids rode.

"You're on," Ted said, smiling. "Did great for your second time. You looked much more relaxed."

Dottie gave Jack and then the kids hugs. "All of you did great, and I can't wait to go riding with you again. Are you ready to go see Kate?" Dottie was thrilled Jack was so eager to take her to see the doctor and wanted to learn what the sex of the baby was.

"Absolutely."

They left the kids with Shannon—since Chase was back home from tracking down a stolen car, after finding it, turning the thief in to the local police department—and could now help to protect the kids...just in case. No one was letting their guard down for anything in the event Hellion or the others showed up in town. Not that there was anything that led them to believe he would, but they were still concerned about it because of Jack trying to take them down, and they might go after his family.

As soon as Dottie was lying down on the exam table at the clinic, Kate began doing an ultrasound, frowning as she looked at the monitor. "Omigod." She listened to the baby's heartbeat and smiled at Jack and Dottie. "Looks like you're going to have triplets. I hear three heartbeats. Though sometimes it can be the sound of the mother's heartbeat too."

"I can't believe it," Dottie said and had her phone out to take a picture of the monitor. She couldn't wait to tell her aunt, yet she had already been getting psyched to have twins, not triplets.

Dottie and Kate were looking at the ultrasound when they heard a thumping noise on the floor.

Jack had disappeared on the other side of the exam table.

"Jack?" Dottie couldn't believe he had passed out. He couldn't have.

Kate hurried around the exam table to check on him. "Are you all right?"

"Uh, yeah," he said, sounding a little rattled, and when he stood up, he looked pale as a ghost.

Kate smiled at Dottie. "Maybe your Aunt Emily should hold your hand when the triplets are born."

"Jack's or mine?" Dottie smiled at her tough-as-claws cougar, who fainted over the sight of seeing their triplets. "You're all right with having three more kids, correct? Not that you have any choice."

Kate poured him some water while he sat down. "Uh,

yeah. I'm thrilled." He smiled. "But I'm making that appointment for me right after the kids are born."

Dottie nodded. "You'd better, or we'll overpopulate the town with the next batch."

"Well, congratulations, you two," Kate said. "The blood test came back. If you had only XX chromosomes in your blood, you'd know you were having three girls. But it detected a Y chromosome, so you have at least one boy. I would say from the look of the fetuses on the monitor, you're going to have two girls and a boy. We'll keep monitoring them to see if we can determine for sure."

"Thanks, Kate," Jack said, finally getting off the chair and hugging Dottie. "I'm thrilled. Really."

Shaking her head, Dottie laughed.

Kate smiled and patted him on the arm. "Tracey and Hal are doing fine. You will be too."

That made Dottie wonder if she was going to have more than triplets, just like Hal and Dottie had.

When they left the clinic, Dottie insisted on driving. "Are you sure you're ready for triplets?"

Jack rubbed her back. "Is anyone ever ready for triplets?" He chuckled. "Sure, honey. I will be. I must be the luckiest cougar alive."

She laughed again. "You still look awfully pale. What are we going to do about decorating for three more kids?"

"At least the renovations on the house are well under way."

***

In the middle of the night, Jack was still thinking about having triplets and how to accommodate them when Jeff came to the bed and said, "Can I keep the pretty cat?"

Dottie and Jack lifted their heads to see Jeff standing next to his side of the bed, as serious as could be.

Turning on the bedside light, Jack frowned at him. "What's wrong, son? Are you having a nightmare?"

"A pretty cat came to my window and started meowing, and I let her in. Can I keep her?"

Dottie groaned. "You know what I said about taking in strays."

"Okay, but you said we could give them to Mrs. Sorenson when people just dump them. Can she stay with me 'til then?"

"She'll need a litter box," Jack said. "Go back to bed. I'll be there in a minute."

"Thanks, Jack." Dottie closed her eyes to go back to sleep.

The babies had been kicking and keeping her up at nights, and with Jack being here for the time being, he wanted to do anything to help her get a good night's sleep. He was glad she wasn't working now so she could take naps during the day.

Jack threw on some boxer briefs and headed for Jeff's bedroom. He heard Jeff telling the cat, "Daddy and Mommy said you could stay with me for the night. Daddy's gonna get you a litter box."

Jack looked in on Jeff and the cat, guessing it would be a black and white like he had growing up, or maybe a pretty calico. When he saw one beautiful red caracal cat sitting on Jeff's pillow, her pointy ears perked as her golden eyes watched Jack, his jaw dropped.

He quickly said, "Jeff, go tell your mom we found the caracal cat."

"What's that?"

"The kind of cat she is. But she's a shifter, like us." Unless there were more of them and this wasn't the one that Stryker had tranquilized earlier, and then she'd run away.

Jeff ran down the hall yelling, "Mommy, mommy, daddy wants you. We got a caracal cat! Can I keep her now?"

Hoping Jeff didn't wake Trish, Jack considered the cat.

"I'm Jack Barrington, and nobody's going to hurt you. Yuma Town is a predominately cougar shifter town so our policy is to take care of our shifters and real cougars whenever we can. In fact, I work for the Cougar Special Forces Division that takes care of the rogues and protects the innocent." Then he thought the cat could be a rogue herself. What did he know?

Dottie hurried into the room dressed in jeans and a T-shirt. She also had brought some other clothes for the cat to wear. "You can shift and wear these and tell us about yourself. I'm Dottie and that's Jeff, our son. His twin sister is Trish and sound asleep. You're welcome to stay with us. We'll just wait outside Jeff's bedroom so you can shift and dress."

Then Dottie and Jack took Jeff out of the room and shut the door.

"But I liked her as a cat," Jeff said.

"We need to know why she's here." Jack was afraid she'd slip out the window and disappear, if she was the same one who had run away from the clinic. But the fact she had returned to another home in the outlying area made him believe she was attempting to seek their help.

When she opened the door to Jeff's bedroom, she was wearing Dottie's light pink sweatpants and shirt, which puddled around her ankles, and she'd had to push up the sleeves because they were so long on her. She was about four-ten, red hair, and golden eyes.

"I'm Carolyn Summers and my family needs to be rescued."

Dottie put Jeff back to bed while Jack and Carolyn went into the living room where he offered her something to drink. She asked for water.

"You say your family. Which includes?" Jack gave her a bottle of water and sat down in the living room with her.

"My parents and sister. I'm nineteen and escaped captivity. There's a man who captured us and was looking to sell us as pets. I found your town and nearly everyone smelled like cougars. I couldn't believe you could be shifters too. Then the deputy sheriff shot me and I was afraid for my family. That they had already been sold off. I couldn't learn the truth. Can you help me?"

"Yes, of course. We have a couple of agents who look into the exploitation of wild animals. Hal and Tracey Haverton. Tracey is on maternity leave. Those of us in the CSF, and even the local sheriff's department, can take care of it. I'll make some calls. Can you identify the location of the place?"

"Yes."

Holding onto a glass of milk, Dottie joined them in the living room and asked, "Where are you from?"

"Originally we're from upstate New York. We moved to Breckenridge last year and then when we were on a family run in the woods, we were captured. The people who caught us must have seen us before and were prepared."

Dottie drank some of her milk. "Are the people responsible humans? Or cougars?"

"Cougars. I wasn't sure who to trust because of it. What if cougars trafficked caracal or other big cats?"

"Some do. We stop them when we learn about them." Jack got on the phone to Hal, "Hey, we have a trafficking case we need to resolve, but with your new babies..."

"I'm on it. Just tell me what's going on."

At the same time, Dottie had a call on her cell phone to Dan. "The caracal is at our house." She told him what was happening. When they ended the call, she said, "Dan and Stryker will handle it. They don't want you leaving us alone, Jack."

"All right. I agree. Hal's on his way here now also."

"Thank you," Carolyn said.

Twenty minutes later, Dan, Stryker, and Hal were heading out with Carolyn to rescue her family. Jack escorted

Dottie back to bed.

"The way the caracal was glaring at Stryker, I was afraid she might bite him," Jack said. "Probably because he'd tranquilized her before."

"Yeah, maybe that'll be the beginning of a new romance."

Jack laughed.

They'd stripped off their clothes and were just about to climb back in bed when Dottie received a call. She glanced at the caller ID. *Chase.* She answered the phone. "Yeah, is anything wrong?" At this time of night, she didn't expect it to be anything really good.

"Stryker locked the caracal in a jail cell and called me in to watch over her while they go to rescue her family. She's furious and wanted me to call you. I figured you might still be awake or I would have waited until morning."

"Why in the world would Stryker have put her in jail?" Dottie was furious, and getting ready to dress again.

"What's going on?" Jack asked, though he had to know who the *she* was that Dottie was referring to.

"Stryker locked up Carolyn at the jail."

"He has to have a good reason. Maybe he was afraid she'd be recaptured by the people who have her family."

"As a human? I don't think so."

"Well, you know Stryker better than I do. I wouldn't think he'd lock up a shifter for no good reason." Jack rubbed Dottie's back. "If you want us to pack up the kids and take them over there and talk to her, we can. But I don't want to leave you and the kids here alone, and I don't want you running into town in the middle of the night by yourself."

She growled and laid back down. "Let me talk to her, Chase. Sorry, I'm not mad at you."

When Chase put Carolyn on the phone, Dottie asked, "Why did Stryker lock you up?"

"How should I know?" Carolyn sounded irritated.

Dottie envisioned Carolyn was pacing like a caged big cat from her faster-paced breathing and heartbeat.

"Is it for your protection?"

The girl snorted. "As a human? Get real. As a cat? For that deputy sheriff's protection, maybe."

Dottie smiled. She could understand how she felt. Dottie would have felt the same way if Stryker had shot her with a tranquilizer dart. "Why did you leap at Stryker when you were in the tree at Mrs. Sorenson's house? If you hadn't, he wouldn't have tranquilized you."

"He was going for his rifle. I thought I could knock him

down before he used it on me. I was wrong. I thought maybe he was in league with the men who have my family. What do I know?"

"Why did you run off from the clinic? Why not ask someone for help then?"

"After I was shot? Are you kidding? I thought maybe I could rescue my family on my own. But I couldn't. Okay? So I came back for help."

"Why my house? Why not Mrs. Sorenson's?"

"She called the police on me. Well, so did you."

"To help you. I didn't think Stryker was going to lock you up in a jail cell. You could have stayed here with us."

"Well, it was the sheriff's idea. Though Stryker didn't object to it." Carolyn stopped pacing. "Maybe Stryker looked a little guilty about it, like he thought he should try to talk Dan out of it. Then Dan called Chase and said he had someone he needed him to watch in the jailhouse. He didn't say I was innocent and needed protection!"

"All right. I'm sure once they find your family, everything will be put to right. How far away was the location of the home where your family is?"

"An hour and half away by car. A lot longer running as a cat. Okay, well, if no one's going to let me out of here, I'm going to sleep."

"I'm so sorry. We'll be there first thing in the morning to make sure you're released. When they free your family, you should be out even before that. I hope you will stay with us."

"Thanks. Your little boy is nice."

When Dottie and Carolyn ended the call, Dottie lay in Jack's arms for a while, unable to sleep. Then she had the notion that Bridget might be able to "see" what Carolyn knew. Bridget had one of those unique abilities that she didn't talk to many people about. Bridget was careful not to read people's thoughts unless she couldn't help it, and if they needed her to aid them in an ongoing investigation and the perp wouldn't talk. She would question the person, and then he would think of the answer, but wouldn't speak, and they'd have the truth anyway.

If Bridget could do that with Carolyn, she could prove the girl had nothing to hide.

Dottie moved off Jack to grab her phone, then settled against him again. He rubbed her arm, being supportive and not annoyed with her for not just going to sleep.

"Bridget, I'm so sorry for calling you at this hour." Dottie explained to her what had happened and asked if she would mind going to the jail and speaking with Carolyn. Since

Bridget was a CSF agent also, she'd know what kinds of questions to ask her to get to the truth of the matter.

"Oh, of course. Absolutely. If her family is being held in captivity, I would hope Dan, Hal, and Stryker are able to free them. If something else is going on, hopefully, I'll be able to learn of it."

"Me too. Thanks, Bridget."

Jack sighed as Dottie put the phone back on the bedside table. "Do you want to go over there?" he asked.

Yes, she did. She just hated that they'd locked up Carolyn. Even if they had thought it was for her own good. But Dottie didn't want to make the kids get up, and she knew Jack wasn't going to let her go by herself or have her stay there by herself while he went to check out the situation at the jail.

"Yes, and no. I just need to get another glass of milk to see if it will help me sleep."

"I'll get it for you."

She loved how considerate he was and she settled back against the pillow. Half an hour had passed since the sheriff and the others had left for the place where Carolyn said her family was being held captive, so they still had another hour to go. She prayed they'd be able to free them without them getting hurt.

All of a sudden, Dottie heard Jack running down the hall. She quickly climbed out of bed and was already getting dressed—again.

"I saw cell phone lights in the garden. Two men." Jack was on his phone calling someone. "Hey, Leyton, we have company out back digging up the garden. If I had a guess, I'd say it was Hellion and Ralph."

"I'll get hold of Travis and we'll be on our way over there. You concentrate on keeping your family safe."

Dottie was already dressed and headed for one of the bedrooms. Jack stalked toward Trish's while he called Chase to let him know the trouble they could be in and that Bridget was on her way over to the sheriff's department to speak with Carolyn.

"As soon as Bridget gets here, I'll be on my way there," Chase said.

"Thanks, Chase." Jack called Dan to let him know what was going on as he helped carry a sleeping Trish to their master bedroom. He'd considered sending Dottie and the kids out of there in the car, but he didn't want to alert Hellion and have him shooting up the vehicle with Jack's family in it. Jack figured it was better to wait for the cavalry and pretend they had no clue that anyone was out in the backyard looking for the stash of money. Which made Jack wonder how they had received word about it when Bishop was dead.

"How many are there?" Dottie whispered as she led a sleepy Jeff into their bedroom, his pillows and blankets in her arms.

"Two men that I could see."

"Hide under the bed, Jeff, like I taught you," Dottie said. Once both kids were under the bed with their pillows and blankets, she retrieved her gun.

Jack quickly threw on some jeans, a T-shirt, and his boots. "Stay here with the kids. I'm going to take a look and see if there are more of them."

"Don't confront them until help arrives."

"I wouldn't think of it. Normally, I'd wait for backup. As long as they don't make their way toward the house, I'm not going to alert them that we know they're out there." Then Jack gave Dottie a hug and kissed her. "Just stay here with the kids. No matter what."

Dottie's heart was racing as much as his was. He didn't want to leave her alone with the kids, but he wanted to learn where everyone was, if there were any more of them.

He stalked down the hall toward the living room when

he realized the cat door hadn't been secured. Most cougars never locked them unless they were going to be gone for an extended stay somewhere else. They didn't worry about other cougars invading their homes. But as soon as he thought about it, he saw a pair of golden eyes glowing near the kitchen, watching him. He knew it was Gigi right away. And he knew that her breaking into the house like this meant she wasn't there for a social visit.

She snarled at him and lunged.

CHAPTER 15

Shots rang out, the sound coming from behind Jack. The cougar fell to the floor a few feet away in front of him. Jack whipped around to see Dottie still holding the gun up, ready to shoot the cat again if it moved a muscle. Dottie was shaking and Jack hurried to give her a hug and kiss. "Go, Dottie. Back to the bedroom. Protect the kids. The others will be coming now." He didn't want her to believe it was her fault, just that it was the most likely course of action the men would take next. Particularly if Hellion thought or knew his sister had entered the house and could now be dead.

"I had to shoot her," Dottie said, wiping away several tears rolling down her cheeks. "She would have killed you."

"You did right." Jack knew from the way Dottie spoke,

she was trying to reassure herself that she really had done the right thing. That she hadn't put them all at risk by killing Gigi. "I hesitated too long. She could have killed me if you hadn't taken her down." He held onto Dottie and felt her trembling in his arms. "Go, honey. Stay with the kids. Hellion's bound to be shooting up the house next."

She nodded and ran back down the hall to their bedroom.

Jack hurried to lock the cougar door in the kitchen. He saw the two men in the garden staring at the house as if waiting to verify they'd heard shooting. Then they ran toward the house.

Simultaneously, someone fired shots at the front door, which meant someone else was with them. "Hell." If the three men breached the house, Jack wasn't sure he could protect his family from all three of them. There could be even more.

Jack moved into the hallway, waiting for the man to break in the front door when someone shot at the back door.

In an instant, Jack was on his phone. "We're under fire," Jack warned Leyton. "At least three men—Hellion, Ralph for certain. Gigi's dead."

"We're almost there. Don't take any unnecessary risks."

Jack would do anything to keep these men from reaching his family. The front door banged open. No one came in. Jack's heart was racing, his palms sweaty as he readied his weapon to fire at the first man that showed his face. He listened for any sounds, any conversation, anything that would clue him in as to their whereabouts. He knew they wouldn't all congregate at one location, which would make for easier target practice for him. After Dottie killed Gigi, he knew Hellion would want all of them dead.

Several shots were fired at the back door and with the distraction, a man rushed in through the front door. Before the man could race for cover behind the high-backed couch, Jack shot him in the chest three times. The back door banged open and two men came in shooting.

Jack fired several rounds at Hellion first, the other man diving for cover behind the couch. Jack didn't want to take the fight to the master bedroom, but he needed to get cover. Hellion was down. Jack didn't know if he was dead or just wounded. Jack moved back toward the first bedroom, and slipped into Jeff's room, waiting for anyone to move down the hall in his direction.

Chase's siren was within hearing distance now and Leyton and Travis's cars roared up the long gravel drive to the house. What Jack didn't expect was for the man he thought he'd killed, to take off through the front door. Shots rang out in the front yard. Ralph dashed out the back door and Jack came out of the bedroom to link up with the others and take these men down for good. But when he went to check on Hellion as Travis and Leyton announced they were coming in, all Jack found was blood, no sign of Hellion. *Damn it all to hell.*

Leyton and Travis rushed inside the house.

"Ralph and Hellion ran out the back way. I wounded Hellion, thinking the bastard was dead. Either he passed out, or he pretended that he was dead. A blood trail on the wood floor leads all the way out the door." With any luck, the bastard would bleed to death before his enhanced healing genetics could stop that from happening.

"Gigi?" Travis asked as he checked to see if the woman had a pulse. "The woman is dead."

"Yeah. She lunged at me and Dottie shot her."

"Maybe we should recruit Dottie," Leyton said.

"No way in hell."

Leyton smiled. "We'll go after Hellion and Ralph. You stay here with your family. Chase is checking out the dead man in the front yard, and then Chase will remain here with all of you." Leyton hurried out back and Travis followed after him.

Jack had a call from Bridget as he made his way to the bedroom to see to Dottie and the kids. "What did you learn?"

"I just talked to Carolyn. I learned that the man trafficking the cats is named Homer. That's the only name she knows. He'd partnered up with a guy named Hellion. She only knew his first name also. I called Dan to let him know."

"Okay. Chase and the others are here." Jack told her what had happened.

"Are Dottie and the kids okay?"

At the closed master bedroom door, Jack said, "It's just me, Dottie. Everyone else is here to help out." He opened the door and saw Dottie aiming the gun at him. She quickly lowered it and rushed to him. "Yeah, she and the kids are good," he said to Bridget over the phone. He pulled Dottie against his chest and hugged her. Both kids were still under the bed, quiet, maybe sleeping.

"Okay, I'll let you go," Bridget said.

"Talk later."

"Hey, just me," Chase said as he met up with them in the bedroom. His light brown hair was windswept, his green eyes narrowed. He showed them the driver's license for the dead man out front. "His name is Homer Adkins. How much do you want to bet he was related to Bishop Adkins and he also knew about the money that Jeffrey had hidden in the garden out back?"

"I'd say it was a good bet. From what Bridget says, he's also the one responsible for trying to traffic the cats."

"Jack, you've been hurt," Dottie suddenly said.

Jack felt the blood on his cheek and the sting of the cut on his skin then. "It's nothing to worry about. Makes me look like I was doing something. Like, ducking for cover."

She smiled at him and he was glad to see her smile.

He held her tight and told her where everyone was and about wounding Hellion, but he'd gotten away. She was trembling and he wanted to put her to bed, but he knew they needed to leave here.

"I've never shot anyone before. But you didn't shoot her. And I knew she was going to try and kill you if she had the chance."

"I would have, if you hadn't beaten me to it." Though he had hesitated because he still couldn't believe Gigi had wanted him dead.

Then they heard men coming in through the back door.

"Just us!" Leyton called out as Chase headed that way to

intercept whoever it was.

Leyton joined them in the bedroom because Jack wasn't leaving Dottie or the kids alone for now. "They're long gone. They had a getaway car parked off a dirt road off the main one. I found a blood trail all the way there. Whether Hellion lost enough blood to make it life-threatening or not, I'm really not sure. If I had to make an educated guess, I'd say no. He wouldn't have made it that far. I believe he'll take some time to recover. A few days at least."

"We need to move you out of here," Chase said. "With both of your doors broken down, it's not safe. I highly doubt they'll return tonight, but we can't risk it. Your choice as to where you want to go. Anyone would be willing to put you up for the night. We'll get everything cleaned up before you and the kids come home."

That was the great thing about being in the cougar community. If this had happened to Jack and Dottie in Missouri, they could have gone to Aunt Emily's place or his parents'. Beyond that, they wouldn't have had any other options except for a hotel.

"Maybe, so we don't put anyone's mates or kids at further risk, we should stay with Dan or Stryker," Dottie said.

"Why don't you stay with us?" Travis asked. "Bridget

and I can offer more fire power at the field office."

"All right." As far as Jack was concerned that would be the safest place for them to go tonight. Leyton and Kate's home was just a couple of backyards away, so if Leyton needed to reach the field office in a heartbeat to help them out, he could. The field office was also the home to Bridget and Travis and a place for other agents to stay when they dropped into the area, and their meeting place for making plans.

Travis immediately called Bridget and told her they'd meet her at the field office when Chase relieved her.

"I told Dan the men might be headed back that way, thinking Hellion and Ralph could attempt to stay in the house where they're holding the cats captive, since the one man who was killed was in on the scheme," Chase said.

"That means Dan, Hal, and Stryker would have to deal with them next. Of course, if Hellion is badly wounded, he'll be easy to take down." Jack assumed with Dan and the others being aware of the threat, they'd do all right. "Dan and the others should reach the house in another half hour."

"I've already called the paramedics to take care of the bodies. Travis, why don't you follow Jack and Dottie and the kids into town and get them settled for the rest of the night.

After the paramedics take care of the bodies while Chase and I provide cover for them, just in case, Chase and I'll return to town. Chase can relieve Bridget at the sheriff's department, and she can return home so the two of you can alternate guard watch," Leyton said.

"Three." Jack was part of the CSF agent team and they were protecting his family, so he had every intention of being on the guard rotation.

"Okay, three."

"I'll pack some of our things, Dottie," Jack told her.

"I'll get some clothes for the kids. At least with the guys doing the renovations on the place, they can take care of the doors once we have a couple delivered," she said.

"Yeah, who would have ever thought we'd be replacing this much."

"Good thing we have a little extra cash to pay for it." She hurried off down the hall to the kids' rooms.

Jack packed a bag for both of them, then he crouched down and peered under the bed. "Ready to go to Aunt Bridget and Uncle Travis's house?"

Jeff crawled out from under the bed. Then he reached out his arms to be carried. "Your momma's just packing a bag for each of you."

Chase reached under the other side of the bed, pulled a sound asleep Trish out, and cradled her in his arms.

Travis grabbed the bags and they all went out to Jack's car. At least the men hadn't shot it up.

They had just put the bags in the car, buckled the kids in their seats when the paramedics drove up, and Chase had a call from Dan. "Hey, you're going to want to hear this. Dan said just as they reached the gravel drive to the house in the country, it blew up."

"Omigod. What about the cats?" Dottie asked, sounding horrified, as sick as Jack was feeling about it.

"What about the guys?" Jack added.

"The guys are safe. The blast took out Dan's windshield and everyone's suffered some cuts from that. They're fine other than that. They're checking for the cats now, praying the traffickers had them in a separate enclosure out back."

Everyone, including the paramedics, waited to hear what was happening. It seemed like it took forever as the seconds ticked by. Chase had his phone on speaker now, and they could hear the men shouting.

"Over here!" Dan said, his heavy breathing and pounding heartbeat reaching them. "We found them! Thank God! They're in a run on the back half-acre of the lot. They're fine. They're safe."

"I'll get the bolt cutters," Hal shouted.

Dan said, "I'm Sheriff Dan Steinecker and we're here to free you. Hal Haverton, my part-time deputy sheriff who also works for a government agency that takes down animal traffickers, is getting the bolt cutters. This is Stryker Hill, my full-time deputy. The men who took you into captivity could be on their way back here. They had a shootout with some of the agents with the Cougar Special Forces Division, and my other part-time deputy."

Hal sounded winded as he returned and worked on the padlock. As soon as it clunked on the ground, they heard snarling and Dan shouted, "We're shifters, cougars, and on your side, damn it! Carolyn told us where to go to recue you."

Jack hadn't considered that part. The family probably assumed that Dan and the rest of the men could be lying about who they were because they knew just where to find the cats.

"Hey," Stryker said. "Put Carolyn on the phone, will you, Bridget? Thanks." He paused. "Hey, Carolyn, we've freed your family, and we're bringing them in. They want to know you're all right." He must have leaned down and moved the phone closer to the cats. "I have your daughter on my phone and she'll talk to you."

"Daddy, Mom, I'm okay."

Jack worried she might tell them Stryker had locked her up in jail. Instead, she began to cry. "Are you okay?"

"Yeah, they're fine. All of them. We're bringing them in. Be there in a bit," Stryker said.

"What was the cause of the explosion?" Chase asked.

"It appeared the men had armaments here too. Maybe they planned the explosion, but I suspect not. I think it was just an accident waiting to happen," Dan said.

"They might be heading back there, thinking the house is still there," Jack said, sure wanting to take these guys down.

"As soon as they see the fire, or burned-out building, they won't be hanging around," Travis said.

"We're waiting on the fire trucks to get here, but we'll keep an eye out for the guys, just in case. We'll take them out if we can," Dan said.

"All right. Let's head out to your place and get some sleep then, Travis." Jack helped Dottie into the passenger seat. She looked done in, with dark circles around her eyes.

When they arrived at the field office, Bridget's car was already there. They carried the sleeping kids inside and found

Carolyn sleeping on the couch in the living room. Bridget kissed Travis, who was carrying Trish into the house.

"Does Chase or Dan know she's here?" Dottie asked Bridget, whose long dark hair was in curls around her shoulders, not pulled back like she often wore it.

"Nope. I left a note on the jailhouse door. But she's safe with us." Bridget gave Dottie a hug. "Travis said you should be one of us."

Dottie smiled at her.

"Go to bed. You don't need all of this stress. Travis and I will take turns on guard duty."

"What about Carolyn's family?" Dottie asked.

"They'll come here," Travis said from upstairs where he was putting Trish to bed in a spare bedroom.

"Work me into the guard schedule," Jack said.

"Okay, will do," Bridget agreed.

"Thanks, Bridget, and thanks for freeing Carolyn," Dottie said as Jack headed up the stairs with Jeff.

Bridget smiled. "Good thing I did because when Stryker called, she was lying on the couch trying to sleep and wasn't in a jail cell."

Jack liked how much of a free spirit Bridget was and as one of her fellow CSFD agents, he looked forward to working with her. But tonight, they needed to get some sleep. Then, they needed to take care of Hellion and Ralph once and for all.

***

Late the next morning, Jack realized that after Carolyn's family had arrived later that night, no one had come to get him to serve on guard duty. He was glad he was able to stay with Dottie so he hadn't disturbed her sleep if he'd had to get up. And he supposed he was serving on guard duty anyway, by staying with her.

She sighed against his chest. "I guess we need to get up."

"Are you okay?" Jack was still concerned about how Dottie was feeling about shooting Gigi.

Dottie snuggled against Jack. "I didn't think I'd ever have to really kill anyone, though I'd been practicing shooting for self-defense after the situation with Jeffrey. But I wouldn't have done anything differently to protect you."

"I'm glad you did." But he really wanted to be doing the protecting. He was glad he had a mate who could do so also, especially when he was away on a job though.

When they went down to breakfast with the kids, Dan dropped by and spoke to the caracal cat family. "We'd be happy for you to stay here, and you'll have a whole town to protect you."

Travis and Bridget had loaned clothes to the family so they could join them for breakfast.

"We have a business in Breckenridge, a ski lodge right on the slopes," Mrs. Judy Summers said. "Edgar and I love it up there. We've been living there for seven years, and we've never had any problem before. I think we were just unlucky to have run into the men this time."

Edgar agreed. "But if we want to retire, or things get bad there for us, we'll sure consider taking you up on your offer."

"Are there other caracal shifters in the area up there?" Dottie asked.

"Two other families. Which is another reason we've been happy there," Judy said.

Jack understood it was probably easier for them to be around others like them. The cougars were so much bigger than the caracal cats, for one thing.

"We'll fly you home," Dottie said.

Jack figured she intended to use some of the money she had for any shifters in real need.

"Thank you. We'll pay you back when—" Edgar said.

"No problem. We have a friend who flies all over." Dan was invited to eat with them. He declined. "Have to get back to work. I have to admit I had some of Mrs. Fitzgerald's pastries this morning. As far as you flying out on a private plane, you won't have to have ID that way."

"That would be great," Edgar said. "No need to make false documents. We have our ID cards at home. And thank you again."

After the caracal family thanked everyone again and left to take a flight home, Jack said to Dottie, "As soon as the renovations are done, do you want to have that wedding?"

"I don't want to put it off much longer." She rubbed her belly. "Everyone's been waiting for it. In the past two and a half weeks, we've made all the wedding arrangements. The ladies all have their burgundy gowns, you all have your dark gray tuxes with light gray vests. The burgundy and champagne roses have been ordered. I've already had my gown altered once. So I'd really rather just do it."

Jack rubbed her back. "Okay, I'll call Mom and Dad and tell them the new date."

"I'll get hold of my aunt. Let's have it on Saturday, all right?"

Jack had wanted to take down Hellion and Ralph before they had the wedding. He knew the way Dottie was feeling with the pregnancy, she would be better off having it as soon as they could.

Hellion probably realized the money buried in the backyard was gone. His sister was dead. The weapons at Bishop's place had been confiscated. The weapons at the house where the caracal had been penned up on the property had gone up in flames in the explosion. And the caracal cats had been safely freed.

So Jack and the team assumed either Hellion and his partner would return here for revenge, or they'd leave well enough alone and stay away so they could take up their life of crime elsewhere. Not that it meant the CSFD would turn a blind eye though. These men needed to be stopped. If regular police caught them in a case of murder and put them in prison for life? Then what?

No way could the cougars keep from shifting for that long. And why would they fight it? If they were going to die, they might as well do as they wished, and they'd get the rest of their kind in trouble. The agents would continue to hunt for them until they took them down.

"We're ready for the wedding," Bridget said smiling. "You never know when one of us newly mated cougars might end up pregnant and have the same trouble as you."

Everyone stared at Bridget, Travis's jaw dropping.

She patted his shoulder. "Not yet. But you know how it happens."

Everyone laughed.

CHAPTER 16

That Saturday, Jeff was so proud in his gray tux, and the perfect ring bearer. Trish and Shannon's girls were the prettiest little flower girls in pink gowns, and Tracey's professional photographer sister, Jessie Whittington, was on hand to take all the photos for the wedding. Dottie couldn't wait to pick out a ton of the photos and put them up on the kids' walls.

Jack asked Leyton to be his best man, and Travis, Stryker, Hal, Chase, and Dan were his groomsmen, all looking dapper in their gray tuxes. Despite that he was new to the area, the fact they all worked in a law enforcement capacity made them a brotherhood of sorts. Not to mention they'd all been in the military too. And they loved Dottie like a sister and were glad to see him taking care of her and the kids.

Even Chet and Chuck, the other CSF agents, showed up for the ceremony to wish them well.

Dottie included Jack's sister, Roberta, as a bridesmaid, as well as Tracey, Kate, and Bridget. Shannon was her matron of honor. Tracey's mother, Melanie, baked them a multi-tiered, white and lemon wedding cake. Dottie once again said her vows, this time while wearing a champagne-colored, empire, maternity gown, but, unlike the first time, she knew this marriage was right and would last.

She felt like a pregnant fairy princess and after the wedding and a dinner of steaks, asparagus, shrimp, and salads, the dancing began. She was ready for a nap.

She danced with Jack, loving him for being so good for her and the kids. Then she danced with Jack's dad, and with her little boy. Jack likewise danced with his mom, Aunt Emily, Roberta, and Trish. Except he held his daughter in his arms as he danced with her. She looked ready to crash, just like Dottie felt.

Dottie finally was sitting down, drinking punch, watching the others dance when Tracey came to join her. "I know just how you feel," Tracey said, having gone inside for a while to shift and nurse her babies all at once as a cougar.

TERRY SPEAR

"Do you worry you might be carrying four babies?"

Dottie smiled at her. "Yours are beautiful. I knew I had to be carrying two at least, as fast as I was gaining weight. I'll be happy with whatever I end up with though."

"That's the way I felt, though both Hal and I were in shock. Ted Weekum was so good. Here he is our foreman and what does he do? As soon as he dropped by the clinic to congratulate us, he left to pick up two more cribs that are identical to the other two. Though for now, the two boys sleep together and the girls sleep with each other. They're happier that way."

"I had my two together for quite a while after they were first born. They get used to listening to each other's heartbeats and so they felt comforted by being with each other."

"I agree. Shannon said she was taking Jeff and Trish home with them tonight."

"Yes. Tonight is our 'honeymoon' night. We'll pick the twins up tomorrow afternoon. We weren't going to do this. Shannon and Chase insisted."

"You'll need the time alone what with the new babies coming."

Hal came over with a baby in each arm. If he didn't look

like a loving dad. "Are you ready to go home?" he asked Tracey. He looked worn out too.

"Yeah. See? This is what happens. You have all these babies and no more late nights out. Now we're just two tired old people."

Dottie laughed. "Well, having been through that with twins, I can tell you it gets easier the older they get." Especially when the mom had lots of help, unlike Dottie when she'd had Jeff and Trish.

"Congratulations again." Tracey gave her a hug, then joined her parents and sister, who were taking care of the other babies right now.

Shannon came over to see Dottie next. Dottie asked her, "Are you certain it's not an imposition?" She felt she had asked Shannon way too many times lately to take care of the kids.

"Certainly not. My two girls are so excited about having the twins come stay the night again. And the two of you need the break. Once the babies come, you'll have a much harder time finding time alone with Jack. Chase is getting ready to leave. My two are getting tired and I think yours are too."

Dottie and Jack said goodnight to their kids and everyone else. Then amidst a shower of bubbles, they were whisked away in a limousine back home. Everyone that had been doing renovations on the house had worked overtime to get the place done before the wedding and Dottie had paid the men extra for the effort.

She couldn't wait to be home with Jack, just the two of them. Kate had said having sex should be fine up to about twenty-eight weeks, unless Dottie started to have contractions. So Dotty really wanted to continue to take advantage of the days she had left to make love to Jack like this. But really, with the cougars enhanced healing abilities, she thought they had longer to go since that was based on a strictly human time frame.

With Jeffrey, it hadn't mattered because he hadn't cared to make love to her at that point and hadn't stuck around. With Jack, he did want to have sex with her, though he said he was fine, not wanting her to feel she had to do it if she wasn't comfortable. But she knew he wanted it as much as she did.

As soon as they were inside, Jack hurried her into the bedroom. Lavender rose petals were strewn all over the bed. She loved her cougar friends.

"Shannon and the other ladies asked me what color I wanted them to be." He began to help Dottie out of her sandals while she sat on the bed. "They told me lavender meant I loved you at first sight and was utterly under your enchantment. Which is completely true."

She smiled up at him. "I love you."

"I love you, honey." He helped her up and began taking off her wedding gown.

"We could just leave it on," she said, thinking she was prettier wearing it.

"I love looking at you just as you are, but it's really up to you."

She sighed. As much as he was always touching her, she knew he loved the way her body looked no matter how big she got. She loved him for it, especially since she was only bound to get bigger.

Once she was naked, he began taking off his clothes. She helped with his cufflinks and buttons, and finally pulled his tux and shirt off. She skimmed her hands over his hot body, his muscles taut, and she was looking forward to after the babies were born when she could get back into shape too. That was one really good thing about being a cougar. They could easily work off the pounds, and they could take the kits with them, when they were old enough.

Before she knew it, he was kissing her and helping her

into bed, his hand rubbing her back, and then her belly. "If you are uncomfortable at any time, just let me know."

He always said so, even when he'd married her the first time and was worried about the babies and the pregnancy.

"You're beautiful, and I'm the luckiest man there is."

She smiled at him and laid back on the bed while he pleasured her. Every stroke brought her higher, his kisses desperate as he plunged his tongue into her mouth and she enjoyed the taste of him, the champagne that she couldn't drink while she was pregnant, and the sweet, sugary, lemony cake that she'd had two slices of.

She threaded her hands through his hair, kissing him back, desiring him as much as he craved her. He kissed her full breasts, licking her nipples, heating her up, continuing to stroke her harder between her legs.

With his fervent strokes, she felt the heat suffuse her as Jack took her to the moon. "Omigod, Jack, yes." She came in a matter of seconds, and smiled up at him. She'd never expected to be with Jack like this, pregnant with his babies again, but this time married to him.

He growled low with satisfaction, kissing her mouth again. Then he kissed her cheek. "Are you sure about this?"

"Yes. I'll tell you if it's not working for me." Though she

wanted more than anything to have sex with him, they didn't want to trigger a premature delivery for the triplets.

Jack had found if Dottie laid on her side, using her maternity pillow to help with the weight of the babies that had worked well and he was able to enter her from behind. Or having her sit on his erection while she rocked on top of him, had worked well also. But they tried her lying on her side this time and then he planned on giving her a back and foot massage.

He slowly pushed inside her and then began to thrust, needing relief as much as he was paying attention to her needs. He was attuned to her—conscious that she might hurt, and he'd pull right out.

At the same time, he rubbed his hand over her belly, his mouth kissing her ear, her neck, her shoulder. Their heartbeats were racing to the finish line. He held himself still for a minute before he began thrusting again. And came in an explosive release. "I love you," Jack said, kissing her shoulder and wrapping his arms around her. He felt spasms in her belly as he caressed her, and she sighed.

"I think we woke them up," she said.

"Do you want some milk?"

"Thanks. Sometimes it helps. I'm going to the bedroom."

Poor Dottie had to roll over to get out of bed. She couldn't just sit up. He couldn't imagine how uncomfortable it had to be for her to have to carry all that extra weight.

He headed into the kitchen, where the fridge light was on in the water dispenser part of the stainless steel fridge door, while she went to the bathroom. As soon as he turned on the kitchen light, several shots were fired through the kitchen window, shattering the glass. He dove to the wood floor, his heart racing. Adrenaline shot through his veins. He quickly made his way to the antique console table in the dining room, moving around the oblong pine table, and several of the blue and beige high-backed chairs where they had one of the house phone handsets. He immediately called Leyton.

"I'll call everyone. Keep your heads down. We're on our way," Leyton assured him.

Back home in Missouri, Jack would never have had this kind of support from other cougars because they just didn't have this kind of network of cougar law enforcement officers back there. He was glad they had that kind of help here.

Jack hurried toward the bathroom. "Dottie?"

She'd closed the bathroom door. When she didn't answer, he feared the worst. That someone had abducted her from the house.

He yanked open the door and found she was gone. The window in the bathroom was closed. He rushed back into the bedroom, looked in the closet, checked under the bed, though he'd been certain she couldn't fit under there in her condition. He couldn't imagine she would have left the house.

He quickly checked the bedrooms and other bathroom. Damn it! No way would she have run outside by herself, but there was no sign anyone had forcibly entered the house. Then he heard someone scream outside near the stack of firewood, a man, he thought, the sound chilling. Jack had two choices: run outside as a cougar, or dress and take his gun to hunt the men down.

He unlocked the cougar door, shifted, and raced out into the cool night air. He ran straight to where he'd heard someone cry out and found Ralph with his throat torn out, blood soaking the grass. Definitely a cougar had done it. And he smelled Dottie's scent. Jack suspected his wife had taken care of Ralph out of a need to end this before these men killed Jack or the rest of the family.

No heartbeat, Ralph was very much dead. Where was Hellion? Had they brought more men with them?

Cats could be so much quieter than when they were running around as humans so Jack didn't hear any sound indicating where Dottie was. But he did hear someone moving around in the brush nearby. He also heard the sirens wailing, telling him at least three cop cars were on their way. Someone started to run in the brush away from the house and in the same direction as the two of them—Hellion and Ralph—had run before to reach a getaway car. The guy must have been wearing hunter spray so Jack couldn't follow his scent trail. He listened to his running footfalls.

The breeze suddenly shifted and Jack knew the man would be able to smell Jack following him because *he* was not wearing hunter's concealment. The man whipped around and fired several rounds at Jack. He dodged, and then leapt over some fallen trees for cover. As soon as the perp was on the run again, Jack raced after him. When he was within forty feet of Hellion, Jack leapt at him and landed on his back, digging his claws into his flesh. Hellion might not have a scent but in the early evening hours, and with a cougar's enhanced ability to see at night, Jack knew it was him.

He bit Hellion's arm, forcing him to drop his gun. Hellion tried to grab a knife from his boot. Jack had no intention of letting Hellion live. He knew as long as the guy wanted revenge, he'd be a danger to Jack's family and others. Jack made a final lunge, grabbed Hellion's neck, and bit down hard. Hellion collapsed on the ground, gasping for air.

Dottie came out of the woods where she'd been watching, ready to help Jack if he'd needed her to. He was glad she'd left Hellion to him, considering her condition. He couldn't believe she'd left the house and killed Ralph.

Car doors slammed out front. Banging on the front door ensued. Jack and Dottie called out in their cougar way near the woods on the property.

The men all raced around the back, flashlights shining all over, seeing Ralph dead nearby, and Dottie and Jack sitting near a dead Hellion.

"Hell," Leyton said first. "I thought I told you to keep your heads low."

Dottie licked Jack's cheek, then headed back toward the house, and Jack raced after her. She still looked like she was carrying cubs as a cougar but not quite so pronounced as in her human form. As they went through the cougar door, Jack shifted and unlocked the back door. Then he followed Dottie into the bedroom where, to his surprise, she curled up on the bed as a cougar to sleep.

He was throwing on a pair of jeans when he heard Travis

call out, "Just me. Travis. Everyone else is out searching the area just in case Hellion had recruited someone else. By the way, Leyton finally reached Mrs. Adkins and asked her if she knew a Homer Adkins. She said that was her nephew, but that Bishop never got along with his cousin."

"He must have at some point."

"We thought you'd stay in the house until we arrived here. You can't imagine our shock to see not only you out there facing down Hellion, but that Dottie was outside too."

"Which is why I went out there. I suspect she was tired of worrying they could hurt her family when Hellion fired at the window and nearly hit me, and she wanted to take care of them once and for all."

"Well, considering how far along she is with the triplets, she's a hell of a team player," Travis said.

"Yeah." If she'd taken the team with her. Jack nearly had a heart attack when he realized she'd run outside without him. Still, he understood her concern.

After an hour, the others reported back. The vehicle belonging to Hellion was parked on the road. No sign of anyone else. The paramedics picked up the bodies and though several of the men offered to stay there just in case, Jack declined their offer.

"We're good this time." He was certain. Though they'd need to replace the kitchen window. But he wanted the time alone with his mate.

They all said good night and Jack returned to the bedroom. He stripped off his jeans and joined his mate in bed. Instead of turning into a human, she curled up half on top of him as a cougar, and he smiled and stroked her head, figuring she felt more comfortable that way for now.

Or maybe she thought if they had any more unwelcome guests she would be ready to take care of them to protect her family. He realized then her protective mother cougar instinct had come to bear.

"Did you jump out the bathroom window, and then shift back, close it, shift, and go after the men?" Jack asked, having to know how she had gotten outside.

She nodded.

"I should have been the one out there."

She nipped at his chest and he smiled at her, and closed his eyes.

At least for now, Yuma Town was again safe. And everyone was counting the days before Dottie had the babies—to see if Kate was right, this time.

EPILOGUE

Three and a Half Months Later, Yuma Town

Dottie's water broke late in the morning, and Jack was one distracted and panicked daddy. Jack's family and Aunt Emily were already there, waiting for the babies to be born. Everyone close to Dottie had been on high alert. Shannon took the twins home to watch over them while the delivery took place, as Jack rushed Dottie to the clinic with a police escort. He was thankful both Dan and Stryker had come to the rescue.

As soon as Dan got a wheelchair for Dottie at the clinic, Jack was ready to push it.

Stryker said, "Here, let me. You hold her hand."

The whole family had come in three days earlier for the big day, not sure when it would occur exactly. But they hadn't wanted to miss the big event for anything, especially when Dottie would need all the help she could get. Jack's dad and his sister were sitting in the waiting room talking to Tracey and Hal, who were there for a baby checkup for their quadruplets. Aunt Emily and Jack's mother were in the birthing room with Dottie, the nurse, and Kate, while Jack rubbed Dottie's back and coached her through the pain. Like Tracey, Dottie opted to shift to have an easier time of it, so she was in her cougar coat right now. She didn't look really happy with him, and he understood completely.

Once she had the first cub, Jack smiled to see she was a little girl. He leaned over and kissed Dottie's cheek. "You did a beautiful job."

The next cub was a boy and he scrambled to join his sister for a meal. The last cub was another female, and Aunt Emily rubbed Dottie's head. "They're beautiful."

They'd picked out four names, just in case, so with three, they had enough names for all of them: Mari, Dylan, and Michele.

In the meantime, Jack's mother was taking pictures of the happy family.

"I've changed my mind," Aunt Emily suddenly said out of the blue.

"About what?" Jack asked.

"I'm moving out here. You'll need lots of help. Oh, I know you have a whole town of cougars to watch out for you and the kids. I couldn't bear to think of all the fun I'm going to miss out on while living in Missouri while the two of you are here with the kids."

"Same with us," Lisa said, shocking Jack. "As soon as we learned Dottie was having more of our grandchildren, Jack's dad and I discussed it and had decided the same thing. We'd miss out on all the grand-parenting again, and we don't want to miss out on any more. We'll help with whatever we can."

"What about Dad's job?"

"He's retiring. He already put in his notice a couple of weeks ago."

"And Roberta?" Jack couldn't imagine them leaving his sister behind.

"This is cougar territory. If Roberta's going to find a husband, what better place than this?"

Jack hugged his mom. "We couldn't have hoped for any better news, for both families."

Dottie nodded. The family would all be together, and

she had found the perfect father and mate for her and the kids. It would be rough dealing with all the babies and two four-year-old twins. With family close by and all their cougar friends, who were every bit as much family, it would be a piece of cake. She hoped.

"Let's let our mom rest a bit. Jack, we have an appointment to keep," Kate reminded him.

"What? Right now? Dottie needs me."

Katie winked at Dottie, took hold of Jack's arm, and he leaned over and kissed Dottie's cheek again. Then he went with Kate to take care of a little matter and that would be the end of problem condoms.

Yep. One big happy family.

A week later, he and Dottie had settled into a routine of sorts. They were glad that his parents, Roberta, and Aunt Emily were here to help out so they wouldn't have to call on everyone else. Of course, his family and Aunt Emily still had to actually move here, and that was another big chore. But Hal said he could spare his two ranch hands to help out when they needed him to. And then Dottie reminded them, they could afford to pack up both families with the money they had stored in the bank.

For now, the family would hang around for a while and

continue to help out. Jack was going to assist them with moving also. However, his parents told him in no uncertain terms, he was staying home with the family.

And he was happy to. He was working on cases requiring online investigations for now. He couldn't appreciate the CSF any more than he already did for making that happen. With the twins snuggling up to him and Dottie on the couch, the babies sound asleep in bassinets nearby, he was one happy dad. "Love you, Dottie," he said, his arm wrapped around her as they watched an animated movie.

She smiled up at him and he leaned down to kiss her. "I love you too, Jack. Thank you for coming home to me...to us...for good."

"I wouldn't have wanted it any other way." Jack knew he had the best job in the world, right here with his family in Yuma Town.

ALSO BY TERRY SPEAR

Romantic Suspense: Deadly Fortunes, In the Dead of the Night, Relative Danger, Bound by Danger
The Highlanders Series: Winning the Highlander's Heart, The Accidental Highland Hero, Highland Rake, Taming the Wild Highlander, The Highlander, Her Highland Hero, The Viking's Highland Lass
Other historical romances: Lady Caroline & the Egotistical Earl, A Ghost of a Chance at Love
Heart of the Wolf Series: Heart of the Wolf, Destiny of the Wolf, To Tempt the Wolf, Legend of the White Wolf, Seduced by the Wolf, Wolf Fever, Heart of the Highland Wolf, Dreaming of the Wolf, A SEAL in Wolf's Clothing, A Howl for a Highlander, A Highland Werewolf Wedding, A SEAL Wolf Christmas, Silence of the Wolf, Hero of a Highland Wolf, A Highland Wolf Christmas, A SEAL Wolf Hunting; A Silver Wolf Christmas, A SEAL Wolf in Too Deep, Alpha Wolf Need Not Apply, A Billionaire in Wolf's Clothing

SEAL Wolves: To Tempt the Wolf, A SEAL in Wolf's Clothing, A SEAL Wolf Christmas; SEAL Wolf Hunting, SEAL Wolf in Too Deep, SEAL Wolf Undercover

Silver Bros Wolves: Destiny of the Wolf, Wolf Fever, Dreaming of the Wolf, Silence of the Wolf; A Silver Wolf Christmas, Alpha Wolf Need Not Apply, Between a Wolf and a Hard Place

Highland Wolves: Heart of the Highland Wolf, A Howl for a Highlander, A Highland Werewolf Wedding, Hero of a Highland Wolf, A Highland Wolf Christmas

Billionaire in Wolf's Clothing

Heart of the Jaguar Series: Savage Hunger, Jaguar Fever, Jaguar Hunt, Jaguar Pride, Jaguar Christmas, A Very Jaguar Christmas

Vampire romances: Killing the Bloodlust, Deadly Liaisons, Huntress for Hire, Forbidden Love

Heart of the Cougar Series: Cougar's Mate, Call of the Cougar, Taming the Wild Cougar, Covert Cougar Christmas, a novella, Double Cougar Trouble

Heart of the Bear Series: Loving the White Bear

Arctic Wolves: Dreaming of a White Wolf Christmas

ABOUT THE AUTHOR

Bestselling and award-winning author **Terry Spear** has written over sixty paranormal romance novels and four medieval Highland historical romances. Her first werewolf romance, *Heart of the Wolf,* was named a 2008 *Publishers Weekly*'s Best Book of the Year, and her subsequent titles have garnered high praise and hit the *USA Today* bestseller list. A retired officer of the U.S. Army Reserves, Terry lives in Spring, Texas, where she is working on her next werewolf romance, throwing jaguars into the mix, and delving into some earlier wolf packs who are begging for attention. For more information, please visit www.terryspear.com, or follow her on Twitter, @TerrySpear.

She is also on Facebook at http://www.facebook.com/terry.spear.

Made in the USA
San Bernardino, CA
24 August 2017